Escape from Athabasca

Escape from Athabasca

A Collection of Short Stories and Poems

Rodrick Rajive Lal

PARTRIDGE

Print information available on the last page.

To order additional copies of this book, contact
Partridge India
000 800 10062 62
orders.india@partridgepublishing.com

www.partridgepublishing.com/india

Contents

**A collection of Short Stories
from the Realm of Fantasy**

Anecdotes

An Anthology of Poems

Dedicated to the memory of my father, Frederick Narinder Lal - May his soul rest in peace! My mother Ivy Lal, Nidhi, my wife, and my daughters: Aastha, and Ekta.

Acknowledgment

I would like to acknowledge the role of my publishers, Partridge Publishing for staying in touch with me throughout, my students who kept asking me when I would be publishing my next book and my readers who have given me feedback that was both critical and constructive in nature.

Also by the same author

Dew Drops, A Collection of Poems: Partridge Publication, 2014

The Andromeda Connection, A Journey in time: Partridge Publication, 2014

The Other Side of Love, Beyond A Shadow Of Doubt: Partridge Publication, 2015

*A collection of Short Stories
from the Realm of Fantasy*

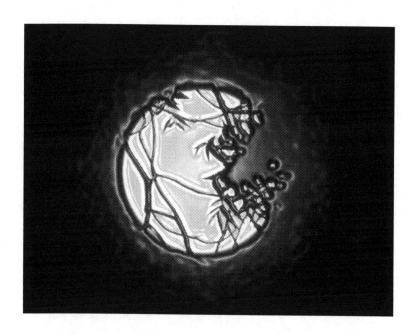

Vellupillai Encounters the Tigers

Vellupilai was slightly ahead of his friends, Thambi and Binu and he heard the susurration in the undergrowth. He had set out with his friends on a Saturday morning to catch fish from the nearby river a couple of kilometres from their village. They had set out early at six in the morning having told their parents that they would go fishing and would look for honey; they expected be back by four in the evening. It had been a successful day and they had managed to catch enough fish though they had not been able to get any honey. The three of them were in their teens, the youngest, Thambi was fifteen and Vellupilai, fondly named Vellu was seventeen, while Binu was eighteen. They had lived in the Sundarbans for ages - an area known for the tigers that ranged the area and the tricky mangroves. His village was made up of family members, relatives, and acquaintances that had migrated from Madras and settled in the Sundarbans centuries ago as hunter gatherers.

His thoughts about their recent success in fishing were interrupted by the sudden sound of a large animal crashing through grass and the shrubs. The sounds became louder, and there was a prickling sense of alarm in his mind that he might be in great danger. His instincts were screaming at him to turn round and flee back the way he had come. The training and education that he had received while going out fishing and looking for honey with the village elders however, warned him not to turn his back to tigers, for he was quite sure that there were tigers nearby and they were walking towards him.

Vellu's mind dwelt on his memory of Rajan, the veteran hunter, village head man and Vellu's mentor who had a trophy of scars and gashes all over his back where chunks of flesh had been scooped from the back of his legs, his calves, all the result of having come across a pair of tigers that were preparing for a mating; he had made the mistake of fleeing from the scene rather than quietly stepping away. This had happened when he was a young man in his early twenties. He had come across the pair, and instead of quietly easing his way out had turned tail and fled as fast as possible. He had made enough noise to draw the attention of the tigers. Angered by the noise, and the interruption in its courtship, the male tiger had pursued Rajan pounced on him making him fall to the ground. Rajan had the presence of mind however, to stay down on the ground face down. The enraged tiger had then proceeded to rake his back with his claws. Even as he lay prone, the tiger began to gouge chunks out of his exposed calves. Rajan's screaming had drawn the attention of his friends and other village folk who had set out to harvest the wild Tapioca roots that grew in abundance in the jungle a couple of kilometres from their village. Armed with machetes and digging implements, the others had rushed to his rescue. The tiger was not interested in Rajan having fed earlier and so left Rajan writhing in pain on the ground. When the village folk saw the state Rajan was in, they rushed him to the district hospital where he had to undergo surgery to get his wounds stitched and closed.

Vellu stood still, confused not knowing what to do thus wasting valuable time. He wondered if he should back away quietly into the bushes. Somehow he felt sure that he had wandered into the tiger's path - Rajan's words kept going round in his mind, 'Don't you ever turn your back on a Tiger!!' He could see the clearing that was beyond the path but was hesitant to step into the clearing lest he should be exposed. He cursed himself for having left his friends behind, along with his machete; he had elected to carry the catch of Catfish that they had caught and had left Thambi and Binu to tie the dugout and carry with them the machetes and sticks that could be used as clubs against wild animals. Finally, he heard the voices of his friends as they moved up the path towards him and breathed a sigh of relief. They couldn't have been more than a few hundred metres away from him. Emboldened by the thought that his friends were right behind him, Vellu stepped boldly into the edge of the clearing certain that he would be seen by his friends who were behind him. It was after he had taken a few tentative steps that he saw the cub! Like all young animals, it had decided to walk ahead of its mother, apparently! He would later narrate the whole event to the rest of the village folk when he recovered in the following words:

'I had just taken a few steps into the clearing when I first saw the cub. It was standing on the farther edge of the clearing and was looking back the way it had come, I am sure it could see its mother and was looking back at her for guidance. I could see that the cub was still young, probably a year old. What frightened me was the realisation that the cub's mother could not have been far behind. I dared not move away immediately lest my movement should grab its attention and it should move towards me out of curiosity drawing its mother to me! What I did next baffles me, but then I guess it was the only option left to me-bending low, I fell flat on the ground with the bag of catfish right next to my head. I remember smelling the fish in the bag, they had already started to smell and would have to be cleaned soon otherwise they would go bad.'

'What did you do next?' asked Kartik, his younger brother.

'Well, I lay down on the ground quietly and waited for the worse to happen, in fact I thought that Thambi and Binu would get to see me, but then I was off the track wasn't I? I considered calling out to them, but then did not fearing lest my shouts should draw the tiger to me!' He replied.

'That's a silly thing to do for sure!' added another voice, a little boy of eleven called Biju.

'No, that was the right thing to do,' responded Uncle Rajan with an authoritative voice which put an end to any other interruptions that would have taken the suspense out of the narrative.

* * *

This narrative had taken place after Vellu had returned from Government hospital in Kolkata. His father and his uncle Rajan had accompanied him to the hospital throughout his stay there. When Vellu returned from the district hospital, he was welcomed as a Hero! His mother had shed tears of joy and after they had all settled down and she had fed him with her own hands, the choicest morsels of fish along with boiled rice and a watery soup made of lentils and a mix of vegetables. Vellu however was soon exhausted and his mother relented, letting him take a nap even as she fanned him.

It was after he had slept fitfully for a couple of hours that he woke up with a start in the evening calling out, 'Amma, Amma, where are you, I am hurting!'

His mother who was right by his side, 'Whispered, Vellu, my son, it is O.K., it is over now!'

'Are you there, Amma?' He had groaned in a low voice.

'I am here!' she replied. 'Shall I get you some warm milk?' She whispered to him as she caressed his head with the tenderness that only a mother can show.

Vellu recovered from his exhaustion after having a drink of warm milk laced with some herbs meant to heal his wounds and calm him. Later, at about six in the evening the whole village gathered at the village square to listen to his narrative. They had all guessed what must have happened to him; nevertheless, they wanted to hear everything from his own mouth. Vellu had told his father and his uncle Rajan the whole story while they were at the hospital in Kolkata, but they had decided to allow him to narrate the story of his encounter with the tigers that day.

Even before he started, he imagined how he would have appeared to another person, a young boy lying on the ground with a bag of still wriggling fish at his head. The person would see a tiger cub of about a year or so advancing towards the boy, getting too close to him. He sees how the boy gets shocked and surprised to see the cub at close quarters! The person looking at the scene would realise that tiger cubs never wandered too far away from their mother and this meant that the mother was close by. The observer would notice how cub was now mewling and sneezing, calling out to its mother.

Vellu recollected how, immediately on hearing the cub cry out to her, the mother stepped into the opening, a rare specimen of a healthy white Bengal tigress regal in her poise, confident and menacing, a lethal killing machine, a consummate stalker, and a jealous mother. She advanced towards where her cub was lying in the grass. Everything changed however, the moment she saw Vellu on the ground! She became enraged when she saw him, and with a snarl leapt on him. Because he was lying on the ground, however, the tigress couldn't get a good hold of him. Moreover, the bag of Catfish that lay next to Vellu's head with the still wriggling fish confused her. Not being able to get at his throat from the front, the tigress turned her attention to his exposed back and legs. She clawed at his back and nibbled on his calves. Soon, almost strangely, she lost interest in Vellu, and turned her attention to the bag that contained the fish. The more she attacked the bag the more enraged she became as the still alive catfish began wriggling on the ground. The tigress played a game of cat and mouse, pouncing on the fish that tried to move away. This was perhaps what saved Vellu from being further mauled.

Ending his train of thoughts, he described the events in the following words: 'I suddenly was aware of a strange sensation when the large beast had stepped into the clearing. Deep in my mind there was this realisation that it was the tigress and she would not be happy to see me lying on the ground close to her cub. I had decided to lie down on the ground so that I would not be visible, and perhaps not be visible to the cub or the mother. But then, the cab saw me and came to where I lay. Somehow, I felt the curtain of my life fall the moment I saw the cub look at me, in puzzlement. The mother then appeared in the clearing and was drawn to her cub. Her curiosity soon turned into rage and she leapt at me with a growl. What happened next took place in a flash. The big cat pounced on me. The fact that I was lying on the ground was what saved me, for she couldn't get at my throat and instead began raking at my back and my calves. She ripped off the shirt I was wearing, and then dug her teeth into the small of my back. The pain was excruciating and I screamed out aloud, after some time, however, the smell of the fish attracted her attention. Soon she turned her attention to the fish in the bag and when she had opened the bag, she began attacking the fish, biting at the still wriggling fish, tossing them in the air and striking at them with her claws. Soon however she lost interest in the fish probably she was also disgusted by the smell of the catfish (which were still wriggling in the bag) she left me alone and sauntered away along with her cub.' Vellu paused for a breath.

Vellu's friends pitched in continuing the narrative from where their friend had ended it.

'We heard a loud scream coming from the path ahead, and both of us froze to the spot!' added Binu.

'And reaching the spot saw the tigress first gnawing at Vellu's back, and then turning her attention to the bag of catfish that was lying on the ground next to Vellu's head.' continued Thambi.

'The cub had fled the spot and stood gazing at the scene from a distance, with what appeared to be a rather perplexed appearance, and then the tigress left the clearing as quietly as she had stepped in. She followed the cub and we were left all alone, the three of us in that clearing!' added Binu.

'I felt a tremendous pain from the wounds inflicted by the tigress and had almost fainted from the pain,' explained Vellu. He went on to describe how both of his friends arrived on the scene. They had immediately lifted Vellu and began to drag him away to safety. They had hardly taken him away a little distance when the tigress returned for a second attack. She advanced on them and they began to shout and scream at her, and when she came too close, they began to rain blows on her. Their blows however seemed to have no effect on the tigress that seemed to have taken offence to the proximity of human beings so close to her cub.

'Our blows with the sticks had no effect on the tigress but then Thambi suddenly inserted his stick into the jaws of the tigress,' explained Binu.

'I heard the sound of crunching wood, and realised that the tigress was fretting the stick into shreds,' added Vellu, as he continued his narrative.

'It seems as if the taste of wood was not to her liking!' said Thambi.

'The tigress simply got up and left the scene,' stated Binu in a matter of fact voice.

'I had lost consciousness, but then came to when I felt an odd and numb sensation in my back. I moved my hand and touched the spot that had been fretted by the tigress. My hand came away wet, reddened bright red with my blood. I almost fainted,' stated Vellu. 'I could feel a strange sense of wetness, and though the miasma of pain and horror felt I was being lifted and borne away from the scene, continued Vellu.

* * *

This rather strange story was narrated to me by none other than Vellu himself, a strapping young man who lived in a village located in the middle of the Sundarbans. I had appeared as a tourist from Delhi, carrying my cameras and notebooks looking for a story that I could write in the form of a short story. I got nothing in the form of photographs and was surprised at the peace and tranquillity that existed in the surrounding area of the village called Tiruvaler. What I got, however, was an astounding and surprising story about man living in harmony with nature. I tasted of the honey that the village folk gathered from the hives that existed in that area. The cutlets that were made of fish were the best that I have ever had. My only regret was that I had not been able to take a photograph of the venerable predator that ranges the vast tracts of the Sundarbans! Looking in retrospect, I wonder why the cub had lain beside Vellu while the tigress; his mother had taken an affront to his lying calmly beside Vellu. When I had the opportunity of talking to the officials of the department of forestry, they told me the tigress was a tagged female and that she was called Amma, fondly, mother in the local lingo. She had never attacked another human being and the latest reports stated that she was mother to twin cubs, a male and a female. The cub that had been part of that encounter with Vellu was still with his mother and would soon leave the group since he was two and a half years old.

Richter scale Tremors

They were woken all of a sudden when the building began to shake rather violently – there was a rumbling sound coming from nearby which reminded them of the aircraft taking off from the Sahar International Airport. Thomas, his wife, Pearl and their two kids, John, ten and Martha twelve, rushed to the balcony of the apartment on the first floor of the Sky Lark building. They had rented the entire floor of the building close to a beach in Mumbai for a whole month of as part of our summer vacation. This had been their summer break as they had wanted to spend the few days of their summer vacation away from the mad rush, dust and pollution of the Capital, Delhi. Horrified they looked at the whole building undulate and even as they watched, they saw the beach approach closer and closer. They all rushed out of the building and reached the beach just in time to see the building collapse like a pack of cards. Perplexed the Thomas family watched as the water suddenly receded from us, leaving all sorts of Marine life stranded, crabs, small fish and starfish wriggled on the exposed sand.

Thomas turned towards Martha and shouted in the now all-encompassing silence, 'We need to move to high ground before the water returns in a tidal wave!' They looked at their surroundings and noticed with horror that they were stranded on an island which was cut off from the rest of the mainland by a mass of water that had appeared suddenly on what had been an open space of about five hundred square metres. The Earthquake had taken place in the wee hours of the morning at exactly a half past six according to the watch that was still around his wrist.

John began wailing, 'Dad, how are we going to get back inland?'

Thomas looked around and stated, 'John, we will have to wade inland.'

Martha snapped, 'Just chill, John, we need to do exactly as Dad has said!'

Both of his kids had learned swimming at their schools although, Pearl didn't know how to swim. Thomas knew that they would somehow have to swim inland and get to high ground before the mass of the sea broke back in a tidal wave.

'Guys, you need to cross back to mainland!' Thomas stated in a matter of fact tone, 'Get on!' he shouted at them as he literally herded them on to the water.

'But what about you two?' said Martha as she saw her mother looking forlorn knowing well that she was the only one who couldn't swim.

'Don't worry, we'll manage' her father replied said as he pushed them off the island that had formed around the mound that remained as the ruins of the flat where they had lived.

Both brother and sister managed to dive into the water, and immediately began to swim with full confidence towards land. Thomas gazed at them for a long time before turning back to Pearl who looked defiant about not getting into the water. Immediately their attention was drawn towards the ruins of the building from which a cry for help that was coming. Rushing towards the mound of rubble, they came across a sight that was straight out of a horror show. It was the younger daughter of the landlord, Seema, (a girl in her late teens), and she in a bad condition, she was bleeding from a hundred cuts.

Thomas could see that she was stuck inside a mound of debris, and so assisted by his wife, they managed to pull the landlord's daughter out. Pearl immediately ripped off strips from her nightgown and bound Seema's wounds, especially those that were bleeding profoundly. Thomas realised that it was going to be a challenge to get both the women off the island that is, if Seema, like his wife did not know how to swim!

With this thought in mind he turned towards Seema and asked her, 'Can you move your limbs?'

She moved her limbs in response and replied, 'I don't think I have broken any limbs!'

Thomas was wondering if she could swim off the island as Pearl and he helped Seema on to her feet. After a few steps she almost collapsed, it was probably because of shock he realised, but then she quickly recovered. When she was able to gain her balance, he asked her again, 'Can you swim?'

She replied, after a few moments, 'Yes, I can manage uncle.' He wondered if she would be able to manage the sting of the salt water on her open wounds. He looked at Pearl with an enquiring glance which Seema noticed.

'Look, Seema, we need to get off this mound and seek higher ground before the tidal wave caused by the earthquake hits us!' Thomas explained to the girl.

'Don't worry, Uncle Thomas,' she stated, realising that we were the only people to have come out alive from the rubble of the flat. Pearl however seemed uncertain whether she would be able to make it to higher ground since she didn't know how to swim.

It was already seven in the morning, and I dreaded that returning wave would come and engulf them all, unless we left the island immediately. I imagined I could hear the returning wave and indeed wondered why the wave hadn't come. Fearing that they had very little time left before the tidal wave came, he led Seema to the water's edge and gently pushed her into the water. He had however little to worry about the girl because the moment she was in the water, she pulled away to the other end, swimming like a pro.

After seeing Seema off, he turned towards his wife and said, 'O.K. Pearl we will link hands and try to swim to the other side,' he said, knowing well that his wife was afraid of water because she could not swim. The two of them stepped gingerly towards the water, but then the moment Pearl stepped into the water, she froze and no amount of cajoling and exhortations would convince her to take another step into the water. From where they were standing they could see that all three of the kids had reached the other side. he signalled to them to move to higher ground, but no amount of urgent gestures would convince them to move back before the large wave hit the shore. Getting impatient, especially fearing the backwash of the sea, Thomas took a firm grip of Pearl's wrist and said to her, 'Look, darling, if we don't leave this mound, our children will not move back to high ground and they will be swept away by the tidal wave which is not far away, so be sensible and follow my instructions, nothing will happen to you, at least do it for our children's sake!' She obeyed his instructions and stepped into the water. She hesitated for a brief moment, but then followed his instruction, Thomas gestured to her to lie on her back and she complied. He began swimming towards the shore and in good time managed to reach the shore. On reaching the beach, they were given a warm welcome as John and Martha hugged them and danced around them shouting, 'You did it Mom and Dad, you did it!'

They all took a five minute rest on the beach and looked around at the devastation. There was an eerie silence all over, and it seemed as if the whole city was in the grip of deep sleep. Thomas was however, in dread of the tidal wave, which he felt was somehow not very far now, he kept looking far out into the horizon, into the Bay, he thought he could see a huge wall of water rushing towards the shore, but then when he stared back intently, there was nothing but the risen sun and its rays glinting on the water. Of course the water level had gone down, nothing strange, this happened during low tide but then when the water receded after an earthquake, it meant only one thing, the water had been sucked up by the power of the tremor and once the shaking subsided, gravity would cause the mass of water to rush back.. Everything was so peaceful; it was the silence before the storm that bothered Thomas the most!

His sense of dread reached a point where he could no longer bear it so he shouted at them urgently, 'Get up all of you, start moving away from the beach, quick!'

'But why, Dad, It is safe here, isn't it?' complained John.

'Moreover, Uncle, I need to look for Mommy and Dad,' Seema gasped, the sea water must have stung so badly.

Thomas was exasperated by their lack of a sense of urgency and he said to them, keeping his voice calm, 'Look all of you we need to get away from the beach, the earthquake has driven the water from the shoreline, and the worse is yet to come when the Tsunami wave comes crashing into the city. You can expect tidal waves as high as a hundred feet crashing into the shoreline.'

Everyone began thinking about the scenes indelibly recorded in their minds of the Tsunami that had struck the coastal areas of Indonesia many years back. The tidal waves then had struck coastal areas wiping out tourist resorts, and entire towns built by the edge of the land. Remembering those images everyone stood up and looked towards me for directions.

Thomas went on with his instructions, 'Well, let's move away from the waterfront. Walking across marine drive will take a lot of time so we need to commandeer a vehicle. Look for any vehicle parked around...' he said as John and Martha began looking at some of the vehicle parked on the road.

'Hey, Dad, how about this one, do you think it will do?' John said pointing towards a humble Suzuki 800. 'The door is open and I guess the key might be around too!'

'O.K.' Thomas replied, and began rummaging around. Delving into the glove compartment he came across a bunch of keys so worn out that he doubted they would work. The owner had probably put them away and instead taken up a new set which he had taken home. He inserted the worn out key and with much coaxing tried to turn it in the ignition switch. It just wouldn't budge, the key was so worn out that no wonder the owner had abandoned them in the car itself. Not ready to accept defeat Thomas kept coaxing the key even as the four others jumped into the car - John sitting next to him in the front. Finally there was a click and the key turned! The whirring of the starter and the burble of the engine was perhaps the best music they had ever heard. Stamping on the accelerator, Thomas engaged the clutch, slipped into first gear and roared across Marine Drive on to the interior towards the city. The houses on Marine Drive would bear the brunt of the tidal wave, many however seemed to have already collapsed because of the tremors that had hit the city in the wee hours of morning. A good half an hour of reckless driving had placed them a good five kilometres away from the water front. Even as they were driving away to security, the fifty meter high tidal wave had struck the waterfront obliterating the buildings and other structures that had stood close to the water front. But then of course they had not known about this at that moment. While driving away from Marine Drive, they came across emergency vehicles with flashing lights moving in the opposite direction the way they had come from. The Thomas family and their passenger finally stopped at one of the shops that was open and sold foot wear, tee shirts and other things of daily use. The shopkeeper's eyes opened wide in surprise when he saw their state.

'Coming from the sea front?' He asked.

'Yes our flat collapsed in the tremors and somehow deposited us on the beach.' Thomas replied.

'Yes, things are really bad he replied with a shrug, the tidal wave will be worse!'

'What about you, are you going to stay put?'

'We are safe enough here, the waves won't reach us,' he replied. 'You too could take refuge at one of the guest houses here,' the shopkeeper advised.

Following the shopkeeper's directions, they reached a guest house and talking to the manager and hired a suite. Settling down in the Guest house, they sat in the lounge and ordered a rather late breakfast. The ladies had managed to tidy up, Martha had applied salve to Seema's cuts and bruises and while the cook prepared breakfast, they turned to the T.V. where the newscaster was presenting a report. The wave had appeared a good half hour after they had left the shore. It was fifty meter high wave and had smashed into everything in its path. The live telecast showed the tall wave bearing down relentlessly on to Marine Drive, and other low lying areas. The houses were mashed to pulp, cars relentlessly sucked into the surf, bobbing in the sea till the air trapped inside escaped. They were all horrified and stunned into silence.

One good thing was that Seema's parents had managed to escape from the building collapse, because of their habit of taking a morning walk in the open ground which was about a kilometre from the guest house. That day they had decided to take the scooter to reach the open ground. Both husband and wife left earlier than usual and had been well away from the house when the tremor had struck. That day they had left at six in the morning and were well away from the water front and their building when the earthquake had struck. Looking at the rubble and the mass of water that had appeared to cut them off from the mound where the house once stood from them, Mr. Sandeep decided there was no point in turning back. He gunned the engine of the scooter and drove to the relative safety of the flat open spaces in the city. Luckily Mr. Sandeep had been carrying his mobile, and it was later in the day that he received a phone call from Seema and came to know that she had escaped safely from the collapsed building. Thomas had a brief conversation and came to know that Mr. Sandeep and Shirin, his wife had managed to reach his brother in Malad, where they were staying.

The Thomas family stayed at the Guest House in Andheri for a couple of days more, handed over Seema to her parents, and then decided on taking the road route to Delhi. They knew that it would be a long drive passing through the states of Rajasthan, and Haryana. They learned more about what had happened from the updates they could receive on their cell phones. The seismological data suggested that the City had been close to the epicentre of an Earthquake which measured 6.5 on the Richter scale. It had been a double calamity, the first tremors wreaked great damage, and what was left standing, buildings, trees, traffic signals, light poles and overhead electricity transmission wires were all brought down by the deluge caused by the Tsunami that followed about half an hour to forty-five minutes after the Earthquake had struck the city. In terms of loss of lives, there were no fixed figures, and unofficial estimates suggested that more than ten thousand had lost their lives presumed dead. While many had been buried under the rubble of collapsed buildings, those who had escaped the initial destruction were struck by the sheer mass of water, washed out into the bay, with little hope of survival. Those who managed to stay afloat, were battered and struck by floating debris.

Break-in

'That is one of the craziest stories I have ever heard!' Harry exclaimed at the end of my story. We were meeting after a gap of twenty years or so, class mates, who had studied English literature at the Sri Venkateswera College at Dhaula-Kuan in New Delhi. Somehow we had connected on Facebook. I had called him a week back and we decided it was time we met. Finally, we had got to meet at Suresh's place at Mayur Vihar over a couple of bottles of Kalyani Black Label beer and a dish of mutton *rara*.

'Of course it is a true story!' I exclaimed, taking a swig from the cool bottle (we had decided to dispense with glasses as Harry's wife was not around and we did not want to mess up the dishes).

'OK, if you say so,' he went on, 'what happened to the female who had entered your house that day, was she ever caught afterwards? What about the CCTV footage?' Harry asked me trying to find loopholes in my story.

'Look, if you think I am spinning a yarn or have gone Cuckoo, well then I am sorry, but all I can say is that I have told you the truth, and in any case, I don't see any reason to be doubted by a friend who has himself seen and reported much more strange things on the battle field!' Harry had been a war-correspondent with B.C.C. and had covered the battle between terrorists and government forces in the Middle-East and other hot-spots all over the world.

* * *

'I returned from office at about five in the evening to the new four bed room ground floor flat that my wife Sarika and I had bought recently in sector 56 in Gurgaon itself. We had asked my parents to stay with us having sold the old ancestral house at Palam Vihar in Gurgaon. The new flat was close to my office and it was inside a housing society in Sector 86. Sarika would be returning from shopping at one of the malls on M.G. Road, along with my mother a little late, probably by eight in the night, she had told me not to worry as she would be bringing ready-made food for dinner. The two girls were away, visiting their cousins in Ghaziabad.' I told Harry.

'After parking the car in the garage, I picked up my briefcase and walked to the front door and just as I raised my finger to jab at the bell switch noticed that the door was ajar! I remember wondering if my father might have forgotten to lock the door after Sarika and my mother had left, or maybe they had themselves forgotten to lock the door. I pushed the door open and looked at the burglar alarm monitor panel that was just inside the vestibule leading to the living room. It was armed and active, but, strangely it had not indicated the fact that the main door was still open! Anyway, I guess this must be a minor glitch, the security cameras must be working! I thought, putting down my briefcase on the shelf before proceeding to Sarika's and my bedroom. On the way I glanced towards my parents' room and noted that the door was shut, my father was probably sleeping, and Sarika and my mother had probably shut down his door so that he wouldn't be disturbed by the servants who came in to do the dishes and the clothes. Anyway, I stepped into my room and shutting the door (although there was no need for it) I latched the door and proceeded to change into a pair of loose fitting knee length shorts and a comfy tee shirt.' I continued my narrative and took a pause to take a swig from the chilled beer bottle. Harry did not interrupt me even as he picked up a *paneer tikka* and followed it with a sip from his beer bottle.

'I had barely put on my tee shirt when there was a loud bang from the other side of the house, probably someone banging on my parents, door! Startled, I fumbled for the latch to the door that led to my bedroom when there was a loud explosion and a portion of the wooden panel to which the latch was attached went flying past my face barely missing my face. I leapt back and fell on the double bed with me facing the door. What I saw next shocked me even more! Walking through the door smoking pistol extended was one of the most beautiful women I have ever seen. She was a veritable Lara Croft incarnate in real life, lithe and fit, body curves accentuated by the tight clothes she had put on.'

'Can you describe her clothes?' He asked me with a twinkle in his eyes.

'My, goodness,' I thought, 'this guy thinks I have gone barmy and maybe he is making fun of me in his mind!' I took a deep gulp from the bottle and went on. 'She was a tall and stately woman, with poise and confidence, a figure to die for, she had put on a pair of black tights that gleamed and shined in the right places, and she had put on a figure hugging tee-shirt that accentuated her generous breasts! She walked in a fluid motion, hips swaying tantalisingly, as if there were no joints in her body! But what began as a confident walk soon became jerky and erratic and to my dismay I realised that she would fall over me. The reason, however soon became clear when I saw the dart sticking out from the back of her neck! The defence mechanisms installed along with the burglar alarm had apparently kicked in! But then even as she drew closer to me I could see the wild fire of determination burning in her eyes! I barely glanced at the dart and instead was focussed on her eyes, so mesmerising they were!'

'So you just stood still and waited for her to fall on you!' he added with a smirk.

I was at a loss for I felt that at least, Harry would believe me, but then I continued, 'I shook off my horny thoughts and decided it was time I did something, perhaps escape from the house before she did something dangerous. I made up my mind and flung myself up towards the door.'

'What happened next?' – He asked me, more for the sake of propriety, and probably to humour me.

'What happened next took place as if in a daze! I barely took in the large hole that had been blown also in my parent's door, but then I ran out of the main door into the open. Fumbling for the mobile that I had in my short's pocket, I dialled 100 calling the police. The call was picked up instantly and the person at the other end seemed to be a decent enough person.'

'Officer, I want to report a break in by woman with a pistol!' I told him. She has already fired two shots in the house, I managed to slip out, but I fear that my father is still there!'

'OK, tell me your location,' he replied in a calm voice.

'After I had told him everything, he promised to send a police team immediately. Relieved, I returned home and this time the door was opened by my wife. 'Hey, Rohit, where have you been? You were supposed to be in much earlier!' She replied in an admonishing tone.

I shook my head, fearing lest the intruder might still be in. 'I did come in early but went outside for a breath of fresh air,' I stated. 'Is dad awake?'

'Yes, he is awake and having his tea with mom in the living room. By the way, what are the huge holes doing on dad's door and our room's door?' She went on in the same tone, 'I hope you haven't been up to something!' She stated in her matter of fact voice.

'No, I did not have anything to do with any of those!' I replied 'Let me call the carpenter,' I added as an afterthought.

'Later, as I sat at the dining table, having tea with biscuits, I was lost in my own thoughts wondering about the events that had taken place earlier! The police had not yet arrived, there were huge holes in two of the bedroom doors, I had been scared out of my mind by a Lara Croft kind of a woman, and here I was sitting at the dining table having my tea and biscuits!'

I took a pause in the narrative to take a bite of the *paneer tikka* before continuing, 'I had just lifted the cup to my lips for another sip when I froze! In an instant I broke into a cold sweat, for there in front of me, stepping out of the bathroom was one of the most beautiful women I have ever seen in my life! She stepped out brushing her luxurious hair, she had mischievous a smile on her lips and eye twinkling and pouted her lips so seductively that I was at a loss! My mind went into overdrive and I thought, 'Gosh, she was the one who had shot at the bedroom door; burst through, and almost fallen on me. She had a gun in her hands when I last saw her!' I reasoned with myself, frantically trying to assure myself that I had not gone crazy.'

Harry began to stir restlessly, I knew he wanted a break in the story so that he could go to the washroom, but then I just could not stop, at least not at that moment, for me it was a matter of prestige, I wanted someone to believe me, at least my old friend, so without giving him the chance to slip to the washroom, I continued, 'My face must have turned so pale that the others must have noticed. 'Oh, sorry not to have told you, Rita is an old friend of mine come to stay for a week with us!' Sarika apologised.

'This is an absolutely crazy story!' he remarked, wanting me to end the story so that he could relieve his straining bladder.

I continued with my narrative, 'I tried to process what I was hearing from my own wife, gasping for breath, my face ashen like I had seen a ghost! I put down my cup rather sharply, 'Oh, hi, Rita, sorry I didn't expect such a surprise!' I said, even as she stretched her hand to shake mine. Was it my imagination or did she really scratch the inside of my palm with a finger? By the time she sat down in the chair right next to me, it was too late to do anything but smile at her. When I looked again at her with incredulity, she winked at me! There was this twinkle in her eyes even as her hands brushed against mine as she reached out for the sugar bowl.'

'Rita is a Special Forces commando trainer, she trains sky marshals for the national and international airlines,' Sarika added a tit bit of information and then she turned towards her old friend, discussing some dress or the other. 'She is a Krav Maga specialist,' she added with a knowing glance towards me.

'Of course, I knew what Krav Maga was, but then I looked at my father and mother, calmly drinking their tea and wondered if my father had really slept through the whole incident. I wondered about the tranquilliser dart that had stuck out of the back of her neck? I guess that must have been fired at by the home defence system that had come with the house?' I said, looking up at Harry who was now listening to what I said carefully.

* * *

'What about the police? Did they turn up?' Harry asked me, still not convinced by my story.

'No, they did not turn up!' I replied with resignation knowing well that even one my old friends thought I had gone to barmy. I went on after a gulp of the cold beer, 'Rita stayed with us for a whole week. She and my wife gelled very well. I however avoided her as much as possible and if she was at home, then I used some excuse or the other to go out window shopping or worked on my laptop with the excuse that I had a lot of back log of work to complete!'

After what seemed to be a brief pause, Harry interrupted me with a mischievous twinkle in his eyes, 'And where did Rita sleep?'

'We gave her the girls' room of course!' I replied. 'And as for the doors to the two bedrooms, well they had to be replaced entirely!'

We parted ways after having finished our beer and the starters that I had brought with me. Harry, my old college friend was as puzzled as I was and he did not have much to say except that it was one of the most absurd stories he had ever heard! Later when thought about the whole thing, I wondered if Rita had not suddenly entered into a dream world and had imagined that the bedroom was a door behind which hijackers were hiding, and perhaps she had thought that I was one of the hijackers!

Sacrifice

The Chieftain lay on his death-bed surrounded by his sons, their wives and his wife of many years. The physicians had already informed them that there was little that could be done for the patriarch so they awaited the inevitable. The Chieftain himself breathed with some difficulty, and there was a pale pallor on his face. For his final moments, he had been placed on the second floor of the three floor tower like apartment which had been constructed like a watchtower, (open from all sides except for the resting chamber) to give an all-round view down the plains over which he had so far ruled as a just and respected ruler. People from all over the plains adjoining the Nechsar hills viewed him more as a family elder than a ruler.

Hildegard, as the kingdom was known, had been a fertile land, with lush green fields that boasted some of the best harvests in the region. People from other lands called Hildegard the land of milk and honey, and rightly so, because the land was fed by a river that flowed from the hills and deposited fertile soil on its banks. The meticulous planning that went into the setting up of the capital city, and the support given to the farmers by the chieftain, all ensured that there was a reign of prosperity in Hildegard. The land once boasted of bumper harvest after another till it was recently struck by bad luck. A blighting disease struck the crops, and to make matters worse, a drought struck the land turning it into a veritable wasteland. It came as a great surprise when even river Chencha began to dry up! To make matters worse, the rains had failed leaving dry stalks of corn standing in the fields dried up before the pods could fill with fruit. The cattle too suffered from the lack of suitable grazing grounds and they grew weaker and weaker their udders shrinking in size.

Strangely enough, the Chieftain's health also began to fail along with the failing rains. The once middle aged, but active and healthy man, a proud example of an outdoors sportsman began to grow weaker and weaker as the days passed. The temple priests suggested a sacrifice, to bring back the harvests and the milk, but then the sick Patriarch refused to give permission for any kind of animal or even human sacrifice. The kingdom had incidentally not known of any kind of sacrifice of animals or human beings for a hundred years or so. Matters had finally come to a head with the Tribal Chieftain being confined to his death bed waiting for his last breath while a mysterious layer of dust made of ashes and dust covered the whole kingdom. The dust tasted bitter, people and animals choked on it, and the plants, trees and crops wilted further.

* * *

On that fateful day, the evening light was fading when the sick chieftain beckoned towards his eldest son, Lot and when he had come closer to him whispered in his ear, 'Lot, take this cartouche,' he said, handing him a six inch long cartouche that was shaped like a straight piece of stick with tapering ends, it was painted in whites and yellows. 'When my time comes, take this to the terrace, place it on the wall and then light the red end. Remember, get away from the terrace as soon as the red end catches fire, come back to this apartment and shut the doors!'

'Yes, Lord, I will follow your instructions to the letter,' replied Lot, as he curiously held the cartouche in his hands. It seemed heavy, heavier than its size would suggest, and then returned to a safe and respectable distance so as not to seem to be weighing over the sick man.

'Lot,' gasped the Chieftain, 'I need to talk to Luna – where is she?'

'In a minute, Lord, I will get her from the ground floor'-and with this Lot rushed downstairs.

Luna had been the Chieftain's adopted daughter whom he had taken under his wings after a hunting accident when a javelin had hit her father instead of the wild boar they had been hunting. Luna had been by his side ever since he had fallen ill and by now she had been exhausted, so exhausted that it took a lot of exhortation by Lot's mother, Tara, the dying Chieftain's wife to take some rest on the ground floor.

Lot returned with Luna in tow and immediately, on seeing her, Chieftain, whose name was Moab, beckoned to her. Luna went over to her adopted father's side by the bed and he whispered to her a few words of encouragement – the sons heard snatches of what their father was saying to their adopted sister, 'When I return,… I will get you married and settled in a comfortable house down by the valley!' To which, Luna nodded quietly holding back her tears, 'Yes, my Lord, I will do your bidding!' – After some time, the Chieftain sent back his adopted daughter back to her quarters to rest, and then he beckoned to his sons, their wives and his own wife.

'Weep not all of your, for the best is yet to be! Don't you know, I am not yet done, there is still one more task to be done, and that I have given to Lot to do. After the task is done, things will return to normal and you will all live a life of prosperity and joy!'

Little did they know that the kingdom would be saved only through a sacrifice, the sacrifice of a human being of great stature, and that human being was none other than the Chieftain himself!

'Yes Lord!' they all replied in unison to his exhortation.

'You are exhausting yourself, my Lord,' added Tara, his wife.

'Fine, leave me to rest, I need some air to breathe,' gasped the dying man, and they all moved back forming a wider circle, giving the chieftain breathing spaces.

Soon the sun sank below the horizon as the family members kept vigil throughout the night. The sounds of the erratic breathing of the chieftain resounded in the space. Towards the middle of the night, the Jackals called out, and then the jackals were followed by the panthers that coughed and barked and finally, a flock of wolves began howling a sound so fearsome and yet the old man kept sleeping. Lot and his brothers now knew that their beloved father had very little time left and they looked at each other anxiously. The night stretched on and on until finally, the shape beneath the sheets stirred and it looked as if the breathing became more and more struggled. The Chieftain's eyes flicked open and all of them, alert as ever, flocked around him while he looked at them all in a sweeping glance, probably for his last time. After looking at each one of them, his head slumped back on to the pillow in exhaustion.

It was a long night, and the Chieftain's wife, sons, and their wives kept up the quiet vigil waiting for him to go. Deep into the night, the wildlife began stirring and soon they heard an owl hoot, this was followed by the cough of a couple of panthers, and then came the most horrifying sound of all, a pack of wolves howled into the night - the final signal that Lot was waiting for. Immediately he picked up the cartouche looked around at his brothers and mother and made to go upstairs. His younger brother made to follow him but then Lot stopped him with a gesture and told him to take of the others and ensure that they stayed indoors while he lighted the cartouche. He also told his brother to ensure that their adopted sister Luna was with them in the last moments.

Up on the terrace it was very quiet, and the wind seemed to have stilled although it had been blowing hard throughout the day. Looking towards the West, where the hills of Nechsar commenced, he placed the cartouche on the terrace wall before putting a lighted match to the red tip. He waited till the cartouche lit up before rushing downstairs and shutting down the main door. Soon they all heard a loud screeching sound coming from the terrace, which was soon followed by a strong wind and then it started to rain. Strangely all those who were present in the hall fell asleep and woke up by sunrise. Lot and his brothers rushed to their father's bedside to see that it was unoccupied!

'Looking for someone?'-they heard their mother ask them.

'Where is the Lord our Father?'- gasped Lot.

'Son, father went to a better home up there in the heavens, don't you see that star, there, next to the moon that still shines in the morning sky? Their mother replied.

'What about the body?' Hana, the youngest son's wife asked.

'The cartouche that you burnt late in the night was a signal to some of the celestial powers to come and take your father away, while he was still breathing. That is why you don't find him anymore!' Tara, their mother replied.

Lot and his brothers and their wives, and their adopted sister were very surprised at the turn of events that had taken place! When they stepped out doors, they were surprised to see that a transformation had taken place in the country-side. The birds were singing to their hearts' delight and the flowers that bloomed that day seemed to have taken up vibrant colours and the bees and the butterflies flitted around gorging themselves on the sweet nectar. Nature as a whole seemed to rejoice and celebrate life. The family and their friends were surprised and delighted by the events that had taken place.

* * *

On hearing the news about the death of their revered Chieftain, friends, relatives, and members of the Moravian tribe began trickling in to express their grief for the death of their tribal Chieftain, and offer condolences to the bereaved family, but then when they heard of the disappearance of the body and the replenishing rain that covered the whole region they were pleasantly surprised. What had been expected to be a day of mourning and weeping and beating of breasts in fact became a day of celebration. everyone celebrated what they believed was the liberation of their Chieftain's soul and they strongly believed that their old Chieftain's soul had returned to the earth to replenish all life with a sustaining rain that made the flowers shine brightly, and the bees to sing and the butterflies to dance in the air. The cartouche had had something to do with the liberation of the chieftain from his earthly body and it had somehow brought about renewal to the whole region. The rain that had fallen throughout the latter half of the night seemed to have given the plants and trees, and shrubs and bushes a vigour and freshness that had not been evident the previous day. Moab, the Chieftain of the Moravian tribe had been a most spiritual and just ruler and his kindness had been an example for the whole tribe.

Many speculated that the Chieftain had intentionally decided not to recover from his illness as it had been known that if he had been well grounded in the art of governance, he was also an accomplished scholar, and a well-known healer. It had been his intention to take away all the pain and sufferings of his land, for he loved his people so much that he offered himself as a sacrifice. The land had needed a sacrifice and it had got one, and not an ordinary one at that!

The temple priests had apparently been clamouring for a sacrifice and it seemed as though the Chieftain's death had been accepted as the ultimate sacrifice that had been required by the region. Soon, the rains returned to the land and the crops revived. The mythological river, Tarna began to flow, the birds sang and children skipped and danced. Lot however refused the titular title of Chieftain, and instead his mother, Tara ruled the land for many years till she joined her husband in peaceful sleep.

Note: An earlier version of this short story, written as a short story appears in my novel, The Other Side of Love, Beyond a Shadow of Doubt in the 16th Chapter when Neena tells her boyfriend, Rohit the same story.

A Space Traveller's First Letter to His Son from Space

The Alpha Centauri Galaxy
5th February 2090

Dear Son,

I hope this message finds your mother, my grandchildren, my lovely daughter in law and you in good health! I am sending you this message knowing very well that by the time you receive this message, a whole month will have passed. As of now, I want to tell you that our travel has been quite predictable. Right after lift-off, we set course for the Alpha Centaury Galaxy, and induced the whole crew into deep sleep. You are aware how deep sleep is assisted by a process of cryogenic refrigeration. This process helps put our bodies into a state of stasis, thus preserving them so that they can be revived at a later stage, intact and free from the vagaries of ageing.

We woke up last week, no older than the day when we entered into the deep freeze. Now fifty years have passed since the day of our launch from the Earth, and you, my dear son are elder to me by fifteen years! This is hard to believe, but then this is what happens when you travel many times faster than light - Time on board spaceships slows down while time on the Planet Earth continues at its existing pace! We have already travelled a hundred parsecs from Earth and the Enterprise is in good health.

To conserve energy we are using a judicious mix of chemical fuels to run the rockets, ion generator, and the gravitational pull of larger suns and planets like a slingshot to propel us along. By the way, we were finally able to use the dark hole as a wormhole as a short cut through space, because we could not have in the normal course have managed this kind of speed, nor covered all this distance on our own using our rockets! By the way, we have also a huge reflector sail that we can use to harness the light flowing from stars to propel us along. In space even infinitesimal amounts of light can propel us at sub-light-year speeds!

Our travel through space has brought us to within twenty light-years from the planet we have come to investigate. This is a planet known as K-55 and we believe that it has Earth like conditions conducive to supporting human life. Through our digitally and virtually enhanced telescopic images, we can see that it is a green planet with large swathes of greenery and equally large spaces of water. Do you know Tom, all the water on this planet is fresh water, suitable for consumption! The only undrinkable salt water that exists on this planet can be found at the poles the rest is all potable. We have already activated the cryogenically frozen spores, seeds animal and bird embryos. We are going to Terra-form the whole planet by first seeding the atmosphere with crystals of a combination of nitrogen, sodium chloride, and titanium dioxide in order to increase the amount of carbon dioxide and oxygen. The whole process will take about two years and during this period we will live inside hermetically sealed modules which will contain homes, factories, garages, laboratories, and hospitals for the total complement of a hundred space farers. Most of the spaceship is formed of modules and a set of compartments that are self-contained and can be detached. It is out of these self-contained modules that the material for the hardened shelters will be scavenged.

Young fellow, I hope you will appreciate the need for my having to leave you on a one way ticket, but then life on Earth has taken a turn for the worse because all that global warming, pollution and the struggle to manage on quickly depleting resources. The only alternative to life on Earth has been to exploit viable Eco-systems throughout the universe. By the way, the moment we have succeeded in Terra-forming K-55, a signal will be sent to the Earth, and then all of you can prepare for your journey to K-55. You will be fifty five years old by the time you reach your new home, but then it would have been worth it. The gravity on K-55 is two-thirds that of Earth, and moreover, the environment will be cleaner and healthier than that on Earth. The life expectancy on K-55 is expected to be 150 to 200 years.

In moments of levity, the people on board the Enterprise call it Noah's Ark. We also refer to the Planet K-55 as Garden of Eden. Let us hope that for once we will have learned from our past mistakes on Earth and make this a viable platform for life. All of us on board the ship hope that good sense and the spirit of ownership will prevail over aggression, greed and ego making us a truly responsible species. I strongly believe the lessons we learn from our experience of inhabiting K-55 will convince people of Earth to desist from destructive tendencies and instil the human values of love and care for the environment, and other human beings irrespective of their caste, creed, geography, nationality, religion and language.

Well this is all for now, take care of everyone in your care. Give my love to Anna and Mark, Marie and your mother.

Your loving father
Mark Cunningham

A Space Traveller's Second Letter to His Son

Somewhere in the Alpha Centauri Galaxy
20th January, 2091

Dear Tom,

Almost a whole year has passed since I sent you my last letter. I am eager to know about the well-being of all of you, hope everything is going on well on earth. Out here we have been struck by a series of disastrous events which have nearly jeopardized the whole mission! These events have incidentally set us back by about a year!

It all started as we were initiating orbit correction manoeuvres that would help aim the ship at the planet K-55. Appleseed, the mainframe computer on board the ship started playing up. He refused to calculate the exact amount and time of burn that would be required to steer the ship towards K-55. It was as if he didn't want us to land on the planet! As if this was not enough, Appleseed began firing the positional rockets randomly, deliberately throwing the ship off course. When we realised what he was doing, we overrode him and switched to manual control. All of these problems started popping up from the month of March 2090 itself. Just when we thought that everything was under control, Appleseed convinced the auxiliary computers to mutiny against us. The water closets would not work, the air recycling units stopped working and we had to inhale stale air. Finally Maclean, the chief computing engineer decided to quarantine Appleseed behind a firewall that he had built up out of mathematical matrices and cleverly devised mathematical algorithms. So far this has worked fine, and I am glad to tell you that Appleseed is now behaving himself. But then all this was not enough, what happened next surprised us the most!

It was on September the twenty-fifth that we saw what we thought was a random piece of space junk, a rock to be precise, heading in our general direction. We took evasive measures and thought we had dodged the object. Suddenly on the twenty-ninth of September, the proximity warning klaxons began ringing loudly in our ears. Nichole, our navigator immediately activated the virtual display screen, lo and behold; we saw a space craft headed straight towards us! Imagine how shocked we must have been! Nichole kept staring at the object so long that I thought she had slipped into a catatonic trance. Timothy, Garner, and Stan were all spluttering and splashing their coffee all over their uniforms. Even as we watched helplessly, the alien spacecraft (which we came to know later on as a derelict) hit a glancing blow at the business end of the main rocket motor propulsion unit. 'Wham, bang!' and then there was the sound of escaping air! Fortunately, the emergency airlocks sealed the rest of the ship from the damaged portion and then we watched as the badly corroded derelict went swinging away at a tangent as if nothing had happened! The glancing blow dealt by the derelict put us into a spin which was however corrected by the directional jets.

Tom, can you imagine we are not the only ones to have reached this part of space - there have been others before us! There have been human beings from our very own planet who travelled this far in space in spaceships similar to ours! I am describing the moment exactly as it happened, Tom, so that you might feel the urgency of that moment:

There was total chaos on flight deck as everyone began to speak at the same time, 'Did you see that?' shrieked Nichole.

'My goodness, I must be going crazy!' shouted Timothy rather hysterically.

Garner and Stan collapsed on the floor holding their heads in their hands. Nichole was the first to recover and she turned the scanners and digital optics towards the fast disappearing derelict spacecraft. As the image of the spacecraft filled the screen, we were able to see the fading letters 'CCCP,' painted on its side. The spacecraft was definitely old, very old and we could see that corrosion had set in, and its skin was pitted with craters and puncture marks where bits of space debris had hit it and some of the bigger pieces of rocks had managed to puncture the skin.

'Hey that looks like Cyrillic lettering!' I exclaimed to the others.

'But how can it be?' queried Garner.

'Well, it seems the Soviets had a highly advanced space program in the nineties, which they kept under wraps,' said Nichole.

'Wonder what must have happened to the personnel on board the craft?' Stan mused loudly.

'I guess they ran out of fuel, food supplies and hope!' exclaimed Timothy.

'Yes,' I added, 'There was no way for the control centre on Earth to bring them back, and anyway, there was little that the Soviets could do because of all the secrecy. I don't even thing they neither had a rescue plan, nor even a rescue ship! I added.

We were all shaken up by what had taken place that hour. A major disaster could have taken place if the impact had been strong enough, or if the angle had been sharper! We were also saddened by the fate of those brave pioneers on board the derelict ship, drifting in space, forlorn and driverless! All of us thought about the crew; men and women who had agreed to undertake what was a risky journey, a one way trip; they must have left behind girlfriends, boyfriends, husbands and wives, children and friends knowing very well that they might never return! In many ways we were like them, after all Tom, space exploration is all about taking risks exploring new horizons – the unknown, all for the sake of the future of our race!

There was one good thing that happened that day, Tom! We were surprised out of our state of trance by the rather loud voice, of Appleseed! 'Guys step out of this nonsense - we have some work to do! And yes, that was a derelict, adrift in space because it ran out of fuel, resources and options. Its provenance is the good old Earth, and yes it was part of a secret mission an attempt to explore space by the good old Soviet Union!' How Appleseed had managed to break out of the firewall was a mystery for all of us, but then we didn't think a lot about that matter because we did need him back again! Appleseed does have these bouts of irritability; I guess we will manage better in the future by predicting when he is likely to get into a spot.

It has been three months since the collision took place and we have been working overtime to jury rig the spare rocket, thrusters and nozzles. We have finally decided to bring back Appleseed online and I am happy to state that he is working diligently. Garner and Stan are of the opinion that it will take us another three months to complete the repairs. Whew, this is really getting on our nerves. Tempers are fraying and we have constant fights amongst ourselves. Vera, the Behaviour Specialist and Psychiatrist has her hands full, what with crew members appearing for counselling and reconciliation. The greatest problem that astronauts face during long space journeys is Psychological in nature, it is aggravated by the lack of variety, boring routines, looking at the same faces day in and day out, and perhaps the fact that they are bereft of the scenic bounty of looking at the Earthly sky with its clouds, star studded at night, the lush green fields, and innocent lambs gambolling around!

Dear Tom, life on board the Endeavour has taught all of us that the Earth is a precious gift which we have squandered away by not taking care of its health. I guess there will never be any other planet half like the Earth. We still have time, and we can surely put brakes on the runaway train as long as the slope is shallow. Once the slope becomes steep, then things will become really difficult! I hope we can drum some good sense into the minds of world leaders that the Earth is our responsibility and because we have an obligation to our descendants, we just cannot allow the Earth to become a dust bowl of misery and despair!

I will be sending my next letter after we land on K-55 as sending personal messages has become a privilege which I cannot abuse. Also, finding time for oneself especially to compose such a letter has become a luxury that is rare and difficult to find. Give my regards to your mother, my grandchildren and my daughter in law. And yes, don't forget to show each one of them my letter. I pine for a photograph of all of you but then I guess that will have to wait till we reach Eden – K-55.

With lots of love,
Your father - Mark Cunningham

A Space Traveller's Third final Letter to His Son

Planet K-55
The Alpha Centauri Galaxy
15th October, 2092

Dear Tom,

We have finally landed on K-55 a veritable Garden of Eden for us. To say that it has been a long journey would be an understatement! Time and space have become relative concepts for us, and to make things even more typical is the fact that unlike the earth, each day and night cycle on K-55 lasts forty hours, sixteen hours more than that on the Earth. The planet itself is very beautiful in appearance - with bright shades of green and blue. Unfortunately the atmosphere is rather tenuous and thin so, as predicted by scientists on Earth, we will have to seed the atmosphere with crystals of salt and other chemicals in order to increase the amount of Carbon dioxide, nitrogen, and oxygen. There are incidentally traces of methane, carbon dioxide, nitrogen and oxygen, the latter being too less to support life.

The Endeavour reached the outer reaches of the atmosphere of K-55 on the 8th of August, 2092. After reaching the Geo-Synchronous orbit, a few probes were sent to the landing site which is named as the

Danakil plateau, a flat area seven square kilometres in area bounded from four sides by moderately tall mountains. We chose this site because the mountains would provide some shelter from the strong winds that blow on the surface of the planet. The probes scoured the area for fault lines, seismic activity and available sources of fresh water. While orbiting the planet from the Geo-Synchronous orbit, we were able to perform a recce of the area through images relayed by the probes. Finally, after analysing images, and data pertaining to soil quality, and seismic activity, we were finally given the go ahead for the last phase of our journey by Appleseed and Mark Venebles, the planetary geologist. On getting the green signal, we separated The Endeavour into twelve different modules. Two modules were left in orbit while the other ten were programmed for descent. We started the descent on the 10th of August at 12:00 p.m. local time and reached the campsite in fifteen minutes flat. The fast entry was possible because of the atmosphere on K-55 is thin and offers little frictional resistance. Things will change once the atmosphere begins to thicken.

The ten modules were programmed to make contact with the surface in a circle with a lateral gap of a hundred meters. After landing, we remained on board the modules till the air samplers and the on-board sensors gave us the go ahead. Remember, we cannot travel on this planet without life support systems contained in the space suits, land transport vehicles, aircraft and construction equipment. After staying on board the self-contained modules for one hour, we stepped out cautiously taking careful steps because of the gravity. It felt a little difficult walking on the ground but it good to be finally on firm ground.

You would laugh to see us falling flat on the ground, unable to stand properly for long on the ground because of the gravity. If you think we were able to take giant kangaroo leaps because of the weaker gravity, well I will say that this was not so because the years of space travel had already weakened our muscles. It felt really good to see a blue sky and the green vegetation that grows on this planet. There is a stream of clear water flowing a few hundred meters from the Southern end of the camp. This water is good to drink according to the probes and the computerized samplers on board the modules.

I finally found some spare time today from all that work of hauling equipment, hacking at the ground to make foundations for the structures that will support transparent domes to house the self-contained habitats to type a letter to you. I have been eager to tell you about our difficult but successful journey and so here it is, the last letter from me because soon, in a year's time you will be with us. This message will take a whole month to reach you, but then by that time you will be a few days from your lift off from the Planet Earth.

Before I end this letter, I want to tell you to bring all the movies and e-books that you can get your hands on. Don't forget the complete works of Shakespeare, Charles Dickens, Jane Austen, Emile Bronte and her sister, Charlotte Bronte, Agatha Christie and others. Also, bring with you all the photographs that you have of the family and images of the Earth including pictures of paintings, sculptures, and other works of art. Finally but not least give my love and best wishes to everyone at home, my grandchildren, Anna and Mark, Marie and Helen.

Bye for now – can't wait to see all of you on K-55!

With lots of love
Your father
Mark Cunningham

Parallel Worlds

All of a sudden there was a shock-wave, the suburban train juddered on the rails, and it threatened to leave the tracks. It was clear that what had been a sedate and controlled journey was turning into chaos. Paul glanced through the tempered-glass partition into the driver's cabin and saw to his alarm that both the drivers were slumped on to the control panel. He had always taken the front seats in the coach that contained the cockpit for some reason or the other and it had become a habit. It was clear that they were all travelling on a runaway train, and it was moving too fast! If they hit the gentle slope downhill, then God save them! The screeching and vibrations seemed to last an eternity. Gradually, it seemed as if the train had begun to slow down in response to some built in fail-safe mechanism.

The suburban train came to a stop abruptly in the middle of nowhere, the sudden stillness and silence engulfed them like a blanket jolting all the passengers out of their slumber into a moment of shock. Paul Gartner had been brooding about Daniela before the shockwave hit the train - a girl he had loved so dearly and believed she would stick to him through thick and thin - it came as a blow to him when she calmly announced the previous morning that she was ending their live in relationship!

'I am leaving you Paul,' she had said while tying her hair at the dressing table. 'I feel suffocated living with you - your pre-occupation with your research and students makes me feel unwanted,' she added speaking through lips that were clamped upon a couple of hair pins that she removed one by one to stick into her bun.

'But why, Daniela, why are you leaving me? I thought we were doing fine!' He replied gazing at her long, slender neck that was accentuated by the hair that had been gathered into a tight bun. He absentmindedly took a hair pin from her and inserted it into her hair securing it further.

Paul's brooding came to an abrupt stop, his train of thought merging with the actual train in which he had been traveling along with the others. There was a pregnant moment of silence and then everyone started talking at once, 'Why have we stopped, Mommy?' And then another voice broke into his consciousness, 'Is it an emergency?' Then yet another, grumbling voice, 'the driver shouldn't have been speeding up, now we will have to wait in the middle of nowhere for the earlier train to complete its journey - darling don't grumble, it is just a matter of a few minute...I am going to sue the company!' They were all voices, white noise, and a mix of decibels, chaos which threatened to drive him off the edge!

Just then the public address system crackled to life, breaking into his thoughts and there was a pause, silence in the coach, an ominous pause driven by a sense of foreboding – 'Ladies and gentlemen,' the speakers hissed, 'I am your driver and I regret to inform you that this train will not go any further, in fact there is no destination left! This is the end of our journey. The power has been cut off and neither New Haven nor Hamden exist anymore, the world has been destroyed by nukes released by a boy playing War Games on his PSP! That is all that I can say. It is each man for himself, you may walk off the train or remain, and it is your choice!'

The hubbub resumed and a few of the passengers fainted while others sat still, turned to stone. Paul could see that a few of the passengers had managed to open the exit and entry doors of the coach and had stepped on to the tracks. They were no longer afraid of the electric current that once coursed through the middle track. 'So the world had finally come to an end!' He thought with a great sense of relief. There would be no commitments, he wouldn't have to plead with Daniela to come back to him, (she was in all probability already dead) and he would not have to explain to anyone why she had left him. It was with a sense of lightness and a final sense knowing what he wanted to do that Paul dumped his office bag on the seat, the tab, his mobile phone, his cards and all those things that he felt were useless to him, however he did choose to carry his sling bag that contained his breakfast and a bottle of water. Swinging the bag jauntily, he made his way to the exit and stepped into the open like some of the others.

The train had come to a stop on a plateau on a mountain top at an altitude of three thousand feet. They had been heading for Hamden which was in the plains at an altitude of less than two hundred feet above sea- level. The Blue Mist Mountains through which they had been traveling towered sheer above Hamden and there were quite a few spots where there was a sheer drop of a few hundreds of feet. Of course one could see the twinkling lights of the town on clear nights out in the distance - the track often veering close to the cliff edge because it was the best gradient that the engineers could identify.

He stepped on to the tracks and walked in the general direction of Hamden where he was supposed to reach every morning at nine to report at the Oxfordshire University where he taught English Literature and a few topics of Philosophy. The laptop he had left behind in the train contained his lecture notes on Catastrophism in Literature, which he was to have delivered that day if it had not been for the turn of events that had taken place. Paul began musing on the lines of his lecture that was now lost in an abandoned laptop inside the coach of a derelict train. 'What if,' he mused, 'that boy had not had the time to play on his PSP?' He walked on the elevated track lost in his thoughts, 'Stream of Consciousness' as Joyce would have termed it. 'What if, Daniela had not left me - what if I had stayed back at New Haven, would I be thinking about life?' He proceeded as if on auto pilot wondering if there was a purpose behind all this madness and the fact that they had been spared from the direct impact of the nukes going off.

Suddenly Paul realised that he had come close to the beginning of a curve in the path of the track about a couple of kilometres before the point where it came closest to the edge of the cliff. The track was now almost level with the rest of the plateau since the engineers had not deemed it necessary to elevate it - the base was firm enough. Then he saw it, a red Benelli motorcycle, lying on its side a little ahead. Almost without thinking he left the track and walked towards where the bike was. He lifted the bike up with some effort, righted it and then checked for the key. Surprisingly the key was right there sitting snugly in its switch but in the 'Off' position.

He sat astride the bike and twisted the key to the 'On' position, and then pressed the ignition switch. The engine kicked in, the rumble was reassuring and comforting. Daniela had the same bike and she had let him ride it a few times and coincidentally it too had been red in colour! Ticking out the very thought that the bike might be hers, he revved the engine slid the gear into first and slipped the clutch. It was like being a free bird, the feel of the wind blowing into his face, scattering his hair out of form, created the sensation of flying - flying like a free spirit, without any care; he left behind the world to its own devices and leaned over the handlebars into the wind almost as if challenging fate to bring on its worst. There was no one left on the flat, it was just the wind, the bike and the wind all moving towards a specific destination, thump of the motor profound and purposeful, the man riding it, a maniac driving headlong towards the edge of the cliff, whooping and calling out in glee! The cliff's edge drew nearer and nearer, but still he did not bother about the fast approaching plunging chasm, (the rider and the machine as one unit moving towards the same goal) perhaps he wanted to take things into his own hands cheat destiny or fate - be in control of his own life for once whether he died or lived.

All of a sudden there was a pause, and everything seemed frozen in time as the bike and its rider leapt over the edge of cliff - seeming to rise at first a few feet in the air an impossible action, defying the laws of gravity – and then, man and bike plunged headlong into the chasm. Paul looked down and there below he saw a huge expanse of greenery spread like a carpet. He was free flying at angle as if he could create a glide path to the town that awaited him far below. He knew that the flight would last a few seconds and then his life would be snuffed out, but then what did he care as long as he had a few seconds of ultimate adventure!

He hit the ground with a jolt and then woke up to see his wife, Daniela at the dressing table piling her hair into a bun!

'Hey, why did you not wake me up?' He asked her swinging over the bed towards her.

'I did not want to disturb you!' She answered through lips that were clasped over a few hairpins with which to fasten her hair.

He took one of the pins and slid it into her bun and wondered about the lecture he was to deliver on The Catastrophe Theory and Escapism. Well it was all there in the laptop. He made sure to add how parallel worlds could exist in an infinite possible ways just like the infinite images reflected in two mirrors facing each other! Could it be possible that in another world Daniela and he had fought and then separated? Shaking the thought away, he planted a kiss on her long neck and she snuggled back into him. Their marriage was the ideal marriage, and as long as he had a wife to return to, he did not care about other worlds, but then there was a nagging doubt in his mind, what if his world was only a reflection of the real world? What if…., no, he would not think about other worlds, he had had enough of train travel and space travel, time travel; he would just rest at home and do nothing.

Flight ET-499

The big jetliner was steadily moving towards the distant peaks of the K-22 Mountains, with apparently no one at the controls! George could see from where he was sitting that unless drastic action was taken, they would soon hit the mountains - but then he was helpless. With an increasing sense of alarm, he could see right through the cockpit wind shield as the mountains loomed larger and larger for the cockpit doors had been left open as the Etartian

Airlines Apollo jet flew steadily towards the mountains on auto-pilot. The first officer and his co-pilot were slumped in their seats, it was clear that they were both unconscious. The other passengers in the first class section were waking up from a night's sleep and had no idea that they were hurtling towards their death at a height of twenty-eight thousand feet at a speed of around four hundred kilometres an hour. Soon they would realise that the cockpit was empty and they would panic. George had already realised that something was wrong, the pilots who had been flying the plane were missing, and there was little that he thought he could do other than to watch as the airliner sped steadily on and on. Soon there were looks of alarm on the faces of his fellow passengers as they realised that the plane was flying on its own. They could now see the beautiful but now horrifying sight of the K-22 mountain peaks, looming closer. He guessed they were barely twenty kilometres away.

George knew something had to be done soon otherwise they would be on the mountains in a few minutes. He was a software expert and recently tested simulation software for this very plane so he wondered if he should not step into one of the vacant seats and take control of the plane. But then he knew playing a simulation game was far different from the actual thing. He came to a decision, however when he saw that they were a few minutes away from crashing into the mountains, leaping out his seat, he ran towards the cockpit which was not very far away from where he had been sitting. On reaching the cockpit he turned his attention to the captain and saw that his head was lolling around. He hollered in his ears and shook his shoulders but nothing happened. Sensing that he had little time left, he unbuckled the first officer and then dragged him out of the seat and laid him on the floor in the first class cabin. By this time the passengers could see what was happening and they were getting agitated, but then he had little time for them, so he rushed back to the cockpit and then occupied the first officer's empty seat. He strapped himself into the seat and then looked for the auto-pilot switch and turned it off. Immediately the plane's nose dropped down. Looking quickly at the throttle control and pushed them forward a bit. The sound of the engines changed pitch as they powered up, then George pulled the control column towards himself; luckily the manufacturers had allowed the elevators to be connected to the control column. The plane responded and began to fly on what he thought was a slightly ascending level path he could see the numbers on the altimeter climb slowly to the thirty thousand feet mark . Next he glanced at the display indicating the status of the flaps; they had been set to the zero degrees which was OK. Now he turned towards the scene ahead of him and saw that he would have to turn to the starboard side or else they would smash into the tallest point of the K-22 Mountains, rock face of the looming Hector's peak. They would be upon that peak in a minute's time. Immediately a siren began ringing stringently and a voice began calling out, 'Pull up, pull up, pull up!' The 'Fasten your seatbelts!' sign had come up in the cabin. He knew it was the terrain proximity alarm, and this knowledge urged him to do something quickly! Digging into his mind for some memory something about flying such a plane, George nudged on the throttles taking the power to the engines from thirty per cent to fifty per cent. By now the engines had begun screaming, because of the added power that was being drawn from them, he also wondered if it was because their sound reverberated from the close proximity of the mountains though he dismissed this thought. The plane seemed to leap, if at all such a large airliner could and then he swung the control column as far right as he could, turning what he believed was the rudder, then he pitched the aileron on the starboard wing up five degrees and the aileron on the port wing down by five degrees. He hoped he was not subjecting the airframe to stress levels that its designers had never thought it would have to undergo. At first the plane continued to fly in a straight line, and then imperceptibly, it tilted towards the right, and then the port wing rose higher than the starboard wing. With the engines now screaming at fifty per cent, Thomas swung the bird towards the right even as Hector's peak reared itself closer and closer until it seemed as if it would scrape the port side wing.

Just when he thought the port wing would brush against the mountain face, the plane turned to the starboard side, flying parallel to the ridge and then turning back in a lazy turn back the way they had come from. He immediately eased on the turn lest they should turn right back towards the mountains instead of flying away from them. George wiped the sweat from his brow, and then turned his attention towards the throttles. He eased the throttles to both the JE engines back to thirty percent, returned the rudder to the centre and set the ailerons back into their slots. Just as he was about to return the elevators towards their neutral position he saw the fighter planes racing towards him head on. Immediately bright flashes appeared from them and then he saw tracers arcing towards him. There were a couple of clangs against the bodywork and then all the hell broke loose inside the cabin. He could hear some passengers screaming. George had never flown a real plane before, let alone one in a situation where he was attacked by fighter planes! He had even crashed quite a few times while playing on his laptop. He had however learned a few tricks from those crashes although he doubted if any sane flight instructor would approve of them. He decided to put a few of those tricks into action, so he immediately lowered the flaps to ten degrees, for extra lift or so he felt, lifted the elevators up by about five degrees and flew parallel, as close to the ridge line as possible. The aircraft must have slowed down perceptibly for the stall warning to kick in; the airspeed indicator gauge indicated a drop to four hundred kilometres per hour. The huge plane seemed to hang suspended in the air, seemingly hovering in one place! There was some buffeting because of the impending stall and the stall warning blared loudly in the cockpit. Some of the passengers on board the plane later told investigators that they felt as if the plane had started to fall down. They had felt it slow down, but then that was exactly what he had in mind slow down the plane so that whoever was shooting at them would overshoot them and on reaching the ridge of the mountain would be compelled to pull up lest they hit the rock face. George hoped to be able to gain a few valuable seconds from this manoeuvre. Initially at least, it seemed as though it had worked, for they all saw a couple of fighters overshooting them and then flying across the ridge. He knew he had a few seconds of reprieve before which the two fighters would be back on his tail so he pushed the throttles up to seventy percent power, and he quickly retracted the flaps into their slots and instead, raised the elevators to five degrees. This made the plane seem to make a leap in the air as it gained airspeed, and it climbed to a height of thirty-eight thousand feet. George turned the plane back in the direction of the mountains in a lazy bank straight at the ridge in an attempt to pass over the K-22 mountain range. After what seemed an age, the plane responded to the controls and now he could see the mountains a few hundred feet below them. They were now heading due North according to the digital compass on the instrument cluster. The plane was now bucking and rearing as it climbed higher seeming to claw into the rarefied air. George believed he had stretched the airframe and the engines to their limits and so retracted the throttle levers till he was getting forty percent power.

Now that the plane seemed to pretty stable dropping slightly though, George turned his attention towards the scene around him. Afraid to leave the controls, he turned back looking into the cabin and he saw with a sense of satisfaction that all the passengers were in their seats and he could now see some of the cabin attendants proceeding in his direction. Gesturing to one of them to come to the cockpit, he turned back to the view ahead of them. When the stewardess entered the cabin, he indicated that she should grab hold of the controls. Squeezing past she managed to grab hold of the controls.

He asked her what her name was and, and she replied, 'Sophia'.

He then continued in a weary voice, 'Look I need to check out the cabin.'

'Sure, Sir,' she replied, 'I can handle this craft in straight flight, although if those fighters return, we are done for!' she added. The fighter planes for some reason had not returned to harass the lumbering bird.

In the cabin George came across a few more flight attendants and then beckoning to two of them he told both of them, Martha and Rosalyn as they were named, to somehow revive the two pilots. They agreed and then proceeded to the cockpit. In the cabin itself the passengers were scared to death, some were praying, the others sat in their seats with closed eyes while two or three couples sat with hands clasped tightly as if it would prevent them from separating from each other when the plane crashed. He shook his head in sadness and then continued to the rear most part of the cabin. The lone male steward was checking the state of the cabin. His name was Walter. George asked him about the status.

'Well, everything is all right, except for a few scrapes and bruises. The shrapnel seems to have hit the body shell although no serious damage has taken place. Cabin's integrity has not been breached.' He explained. 'By the way you seemed to have handled the situation like a pro, Sir!' He said, and then after a pause he went on, 'Have you flown a plane before, Sir?' He asked George.

George thought carefully before replying he didn't want Walter to panic thinking he couldn't fly the plane so he stated, 'I have two hundred hours on simulators, various aircraft' he stated not desiring to be party to lie. When Walter nodded his head, in approval, he continued, 'Fine I will return to the cockpit and see how things are going there,' and proceeded back to the cockpit.

At the cockpit, Sophia had managed to maintain a fairly level flight. She turned to him anxiously and said, 'Sir would you like to take over the controls?'

'No you carry on right now,' George added viewing the panorama of snow covered mountains stretching below them. Presently the speakers crackled hissed and then a voice came through:

'Alpha Tango Foxtrot two-two, come in, do you hear me? Please respond, this the Lintz control tower, you are overdue at check point Charlie!'

George looked dubiously at Sophia, but then she flicked a switch in front of her and replied, 'Check point Charlie, we have had an incident!' She identified herself and then went on to describe how the pilots had become unconscious, the plane had nearly dashed into the K-22 mountain range, and then been fired upon by two fighter planes. Sophia described how George had taken control of the plane and had managed to fly over the mountain top. The man at the control tower seemed incredulous and asked to talk to George.

Sophia then indicated that he put on the headphones and then pointed towards the relevant button he needed to press to speak and listen to the tower. The man at the other end introduced himself as Tony and then went on to ask George if he had any experience in flying planes. George replied that he had tested a flight simulator software for flying that plane on his laptop and that apart from that he had had no practical experience! Tony took some time to digest this information. He then told George to maintain course as he would be calling experts from the consortium that had manufactured the aircraft. Tony added that he would contact the aircraft in exactly half an hour's time.

It was already getting late and it was three in the evening, a good five hours after they had been attacked by the fighter planes.

True to Tony's promise, the radio crackled exactly within the half hour. 'Alpha Tango Foxtrot two-two come in, report status of fuel and flight parameters!'

George flicked the switch, 'Hello, check point Charlie, this is George here, in control of aircraft Alpha Tango foxtrot, two-two!'

The speaker crackled in reply, 'Mr George, this is chief aeronautical engineer, and designer for the plane you are flying, Wolfgang Schmitz, please check the fuel gauge reading.'

'Twenty thousand gallons are remaining!'- George replied.

'What is the reading on the airspeed gauge?'

'The airspeed is 400 kilometres per hour.' He responded, stating the metric value.

'Please read out the aircraft heading on the GPS?'

'90 degrees due North West,' He added.

'Fine, you are doing OK and what about the altitude?'

'Thirty-two thousand feet,' George replied.

The conversation went on for about fifteen minutes and then the man at the other end began instructing him about the programming of the on-board computer. They went on and on till at last the he had been done everything as instructed. Finally Mr Schmitz told him to switch on the autopilot as instructed. George acquiesced and then he stepped into the second officer's seat.

After a radio silence of a few minutes, which seemed to last ages, Mr Schmitz came back on line and then he instructed George to somehow revive at least one of the flying officers.

George stepped out of the cockpit and then indicated to one of the stewardesses to help him revive the first officer.

Tanya, the stewardess told him that she had had some training in this sort of problem and at once she began injecting him with some medicine from the vials she carried in her vanity bag. Soon the First Officer, Gustav Benjamin as his nameplate read revived from his deep sleep and then immediately remembering that he should be at the controls lurched towards the cockpit. He had barely taken a few steps before he collapsed on the floor. The first officer gazed helplessly at both, George and Tanya who lifted him back into one of the vacant seats in the first class section of the cabin. A good ten minutes had elapsed before Gustav recovered sufficiently enough. George informed him about the situation, and hearing the status, the first officer told them to take him to his seat in the cockpit. Once there, they strapped him into his seat. Sophia had earlier stepped out of the first officer's seat when she saw them approach. The pilot and the stewardess exchanged smiles and then Mr Gustav took over the controls. He indicated to George that he should take the second officer's seat. Sophia and George then lifted the limp body of the co-pilot and then dragged him to George's seat in the first class cabin. He then returned to the cockpit where he took the second officer's seat. Gustav, the now fully recovered contacted the control tower and told them that although he was still feeling dizzy after consuming the cup of soup that had apparently been spiked with drugs he was good to go. He also mentioned that he would be assisted by George whom he would instruct accordingly. Together, both first Officer Gustav and George managed to fly the plane and then land it at one of the mountain resort airports at Lintz. Even as they approached the runway for a landing, they could see the emergency vehicles, ambulances fire tenders with flashing beacons waiting for them along the runway. The landing when it took place had been uneventful except for the cheering of the passengers. The passengers disembarked through the usual exits. The two men in the cockpit however collapsed in their seats, Gustav from the lingering after effects of the drug that had been put into his coffee, while George collapsed with sheer exhaustion. They were taken out of the plane on stretchers along with the second officer Boris Lysenko whom the cabin crew had not been able to revive fully.

The destination of the plane had been the city of Bloomberg in the Alps but then the incident had caused a diversion to the mountain top airport at Lintz. The passengers were lodged at the famous alpine resort hotel known as Alpine Heights hotel. They were to be taken to their final destination by a special plane. George and the two pilots were part of the compliment of the plane albeit as passengers.

When the aircraft investigators accompanied by reporters revisited the aircraft for an inspection, they were amazed to see that shrapnel from the fighter planes had indeed struck the plane in a dozen different places but had somehow not managed to puncture the skin!

The newspapers and the news channels described the incident in great detail for about two weeks and then they too switched to other burning topics like the attacking of freight ships in the Gulf of Aden by pirates, and the shooting down of an Andoran air force plane over the Strait of Hormuz. As for George, well he was glad to be re-united with his fiancée Rosa whom he would marry in a couple of months' time. Mr Gustav and Mr Boris were guests of honour at a low key and private marriage ceremony that took place in the town of Lintz, close to the place where the plane had finally landed successfully. Investigations into the strange incident of flight ET-499 are still going on. One of the greatest mysteries however was how the coffee served to the two pilots happened to be spiked with drugs. No one knows who the culprits were, no one knows why the fighter planes had shot at Flight ET-499, nor does anyone know to which country they had belonged to.

Shalini

S he had gathered an assorted group of listeners, young and old, all cousins waiting for what they thought was going to be a juicy story. She was Tarini, their college going cousin sister and she was the eldest among them.

It had been a custom for all the cousins to gather at their aunt's house in Delhi, and to listen to a story by their cousin sister Tarini. Little did they know that the story they were going to hear that day was going to be one they would never forget all their lives, it was a story that would challenge their philosophy of life - it would stir their minds to higher levels of imagination and fantasy and force them to question their beliefs in the afterlife, and ghosts and hauntings. I wouldn't like to spill the beans at the outset and so I will continue with the story that I heard many years ago.

The incidents in this story had taken place in a normal home in Sadiq Nagar in Delhi when the lady of the house had fallen ill all of a sudden. The doctors at the Holy Family hospital diagnosed the disease and told her husband that his wife had Leukaemia and she had few days of life left. Her last days were rather disturbed, waking up in the middle of the night, gasping and struggling for breath, that sinking feeling, as if she was drowning in a sea. Shalini Sharma was attended by her two daughters, Rekha and Mansi, fourteen and sixteen. She had a loving and devoted husband, Vineet, who was a family man who loved his wife a lot. Mr. Vineet Sharma was a managing director in a firm that dealt in office automation and peripherals. He had sources in good hospitals, but unfortunately, Shalini was past recovery. When Vineet met a few doctors and suggested that they perform a bone marrow transplant on his wife, they refused looking at the stage at which the disease had progressed. After a few days, the doctors at the hospital where she had been admitted advised Vineet to take Shalini back home so that she could be with her loved ones in her last days. My cousin sister took a pause before continuing with the story.

'Rekha was especially close to her mother, after school and throughout the night she was Shalini's side. It was not that Mansi was not close to her mother, it was just that she was a little shy about expressing her feelings towards others. Mansi was aware even late at night of the times when her mother called out in pain and Rekha was not able to respond because she had fallen asleep due to exhaustion. She would step in and do whatever was required to help her mother out.

Shalini lived all of two months after she had been diagnosed with terminal Leukaemia. The cancer had finally spread all over her body, infecting her organs, and her bones. Life had become very painful for her although she tried to present a smiling face towards the rest of her family. She had been a dynamic, cheerful woman in her better days, and although she tried to present a brave face, it was clear that she was suffering. What made her feel even worse emotionally was that she felt ashamed about her dependence on others for now she had barely any control over her bowel movements. She often slipped into a disturbed sleep only to wake up crying out in pain. The days were relatively peaceful but it was the nights that Shalini feared the most because it was during the night that she felt the dark shadows drawing in.

She had been an English teacher at a nearby school, the life and joy of the entire grade eleven and grade twelve students that she taught. She went for morning walks, did yoga, and even rode Rekha's bicycle to the market although her daughters often scolded her and told her to take and auto. Lean and athletic in build, Shalini had been a power house of energy. She looked after the household with great efficiency, cooked meals for the family, ran errands, and taught her two daughters Maths and English. Shalini was a devout Hindu and she went to the temple regularly. She respected all religions and once when Mansi had fallen ill with Pneumonia (when she was twelve), she had gone to Temples, Gurudwaras, and Churches to pray for her daughter's recovery. It seemed as if her prayers had been accepted when Mansi finally bounced back from her ailment.

Initially at least, Shalini continued to try looking after the family when she returned from the hospital after being diagnosed with terminal cancer. Shalini had not known what she was suffering from and thought that it might have been only a viral fever. She managed the cooking and a few more chores, although she could not manage the errands to the local market to get vegetables because it had become very tiring. Things became serious when a couple of weeks after her return from the hospital, she had been cooking lunch when she collapsed on the kitchen floor and was found by her daughters when they returned from school. The food in the cooker had burned to cinders, and as she lay so motionless on the floor that the two girls thought she had finally passed away. Rekha began screaming with anguish as her elder sister tried to pull her away, but then Shalini suddenly recovered and sat up, shaking away the feeling of lethargy that had engulfed her.

The doctors had prescribed medicines to make her pain more bearable, but Shalini refused to take them even when the nurse who visited her once a day insisted that she should. About three weeks after she had returned from hospital, Shalini was forced to accept defeat; that she would now have to confine herself to her bed. She felt ashamed for not being able to go the toilet and had to use the bed pan. Shalini could see how life was slipping away from her, and saw that she would not be around to see her two daughters now developing into smart women, as future homemakers and mothers. What pained her most was not the physical pain that she felt deep inside her body, but the pain of a realisation that she that she would not be around when her daughters most needed her, problems with boyfriends, broken relationships, marriage, childbirth, and the joy of having her daughters to visit her after their marriage.

Somehow it was as if she did not want to let go of life and she struggled against all odds, defying the doctor's prediction that she would live all of three weeks. Her tenacity in clinging to life meant that she wouldn't go easily and peacefully. A month passed away and Shalini was still there, greeting her family members each morning albeit in a steadily weakening voice, becoming a mere husk of a human body shrinking into its skeleton. By the fifth week of her return from the hospital, she lay quietly, lost in her thoughts. Her lovely complexion, her skin, had begun to turn a disturbing black. She was but a shade of her chirpy self and could no longer entertain others with her wit. But then she just lingered on, her two daughters attending to her, her husband always by her side – they were all waiting for her to go, they knew she was on her last legs, but then she would not go!

During her last days, she was visited by a priest from a close by church, a pundit, and the priest from the Gurudwara. They were all young men who were full of life, and when they visited her often meeting each other with camaraderie, they were all united in their knowledge that she was fighting death. The priest read verses from the Bible, while the pundit read from the Gita, and the priest from the Gurudwara read verses from the Holy Writ. The loud readings from the scriptures gave her a sense of peacefulness but then the problem was that listening to the verses from the holy scriptures made her feel as if she was about to set out on her last journey. The fact was that she just did not want to let go of life! She thought she had unfinished work and simply clung on to life even though the messenger of death was there to take her away.

Her last days were very painful; she could not digest any solids. Whatever she ate was voided moments after she had swallowed it. The doctor came to visit her everyday now and he recommended a liquid diet. Very quietly, lest she should hear him, he told her husband that she could slip away any moment now.

But, then Shalini's hold on life was a tenacious one and she struggled on, dragging in painful breath after painful breath. Her two daughters were constantly by her side, and her eyes filled with tears when she looked at them, concerned, empathetic, always by the bedside, ever ready with sponge towels spoons to feed her sips of water and juice and whatever they could give her that would not be rejected by her body. By now, her complexion had turned black, her eyes had sunken into their hollows and what had once been a beautiful face was now a sight for sore eyes. The nurse who came once a day told Vineet and the two girls that Shalini was suffering a lot from pain and that the only medicine she could give her was morphine. However the moment she tried to insert the needle, Shalini woke up and asked if it was morphine. When the nurse replied in the affirmative, she told her that she wanted to remain awake and alert so that she could savour her last moments. The nurse acquiesced, out of a respect for the dying woman.

Finally, one fine day, it was a Saturday, and the month was October, Shalini left her family for a heavenly abode. The cremation took place that very day at *Nigam Bodh Ghat*, and the house was now full of grieving relatives and friends. Vineet was inconsolable, and surprisingly, the two girls had taken things into their hands and managed very well. It finally looked like life would finally settle down and return to normal at the Sharmas. Vineet's mother and father shifted base from Chandigarh and they began living with their son and two granddaughters in the Sadiq Nagar flat. The month of November passed away smoothly and everyone thought that the worst had passed away, but that was not to be! Shalini's soul was not at peace after all!

It was in the month of December that Rekha began having nightmares. She would wake up in the middle of the night and then start shrieking and screaming, and when she quieted down she began speaking in Shalini's voice. Vineet decided to do something about this and so he took his younger daughter to a Psychiatrist in South Extension. The psychiatrist diagnosed the problem as PTSD and he prescribed bed rest and some mild relaxants there were to be taken regularly. Just when things seemed to be returning to normal, Rekha had her first seizure on the twentieth. Her father rushed her to another Doctor who, after a few tests confirmed that Rekha was having severe epileptic fits. Medicines were prescribed and it seemed as though Rekha would recover in due time, but then, again this was not to be!

Even after taking the medicines, Rekha's condition continued to deteriorate. The pundit, priest from the nearby church and Gurudwara began turning up. One day while the priest from the Gurudwara and the pastor from the nearby Church were praying together in turns for the wellbeing of Rekha, she had another of those attacks. At first they felt the bed shake and then they felt the little girl seem to rise from her bed, but then not yet ready to open their eyes as they believed there was something wrong going on and they were afraid to see it! While the Church Priest prayed and the priest from the Gurudwara listened, they could sense a change coming into Rekha, malevolence filled with destructive energy that seemed to flow from the girl's body and filled the room. The two religious men wanted to flee, but then the pastor was not yet done, and even as both men prayed, Rekha stepped off the bed, and then snatched the Holy writ from the pastor's hands and tore it into two, and then she slapped both the men really hard. Now they could no longer keep their eyes shut, and so when they opened their eyes they were frightened out of their wits to see the fierce, bloodshot eyes that seemed bored fiery holes into them. Before the two men could recover from their shock, she spoke:

'Who do you think you are trying to fool both of you?' she addressed them, her voice strangely calm; it was the voice of Shalini.

The pastor was the first to respond, and he said in a steady voice, trying to keep the tremor out, 'Shalini, why don't to go away, there is a better place waiting for you up there!'

To which the girl replied, 'Pastor, how dare to banish me from this world, don't you know my work is not yet done, this was not the right time for me to go, Rekha needs my help, I cannot leave her, and please don't interfere in our family matters, both of you.'

The priest from the nearby Gurudwara decided to intervene and he said, 'Shalini, you know you cannot remain on this earth, you are dead, you need to let go, leave your daughter, and let her be herself!'

It was clear to both the clerics that this was a case the mother's soul invading another body, in this case her own daughter's body in an effort to linger on. Shalini had not wanted to let go, and she thought she had a lot of unfinished work to do. She had died, she believed, and untimely death.

Listening to this, the girl blew up in rage, she began convulsing, she was in the grip of yet another fit, and she raged and shouted at them through a mouth filled with blood, for she had bitten her tongue, 'Get lost both of you, you fools, wasting the time of busy people with all this nonsense of life after death. Remember, there is nothing but hell, hell on earth and hell after death that is the reality!' she screamed even as she lunged at the two men who turned towards the door to flee.'

Later when they had the time to meet together, the priest from the Gurudwara and the Pastor who were close friends would express surprise that Shalini should speak so rudely to them. She had been a regular visitor at the Gurudwara and the Church and had spoken to both of them whenever she visited the places of worship.

* * *

It was past midnight, and yet none of us listeners was really sleepy, and we did get up to visit the loo or have a drink of water. My aunt stepped out of her room and told us it was high time we went off to sleep. We then assured her that there was just half an hour of story left and she nodded and returned to her room. By the time we all settled once more, it was already one o'clock! We all knew it was high time we slept, but then we wanted to hear the rest of the story! The interest had shifted from Shalini, to her daughter Rekha.

'Well,' my cousin sister resumed, 'Mr. Vineet Sharma took his daughter to some of the best doctors in the city, and when he asked them if it was a case of possession, they scoffed at him saying that there was no such thing in their profession at least! A few months into the treatment, however, there was no improvement in Rekha's condition and by now both grandparents, Vineet, and Mansi were clearly worried. They could see that something was eating Rekha from inside, the once chubby and stout girl had become a skeleton, and like her mother, she had turned black, her eyes sunk into hollows, making her look like a monster.

Finally the solution presented itself out of the blue. There was a knock on their door, and when Mansi opened the door, there standing outside was a wizened old man looking at her.

'What do you want, Babaji,' asked Mansi.

'To have something to eat and something to drink, I am thirsty and hungry, I have been travelling for quite some time now,' he replied.

'Sure, Babaji,' Mansi replied and re-entered the house to get some water and some food. She stepped out of the house and gave the man some water and served him the food which consisted of rice, lentils and some vegetables. These he ate carefully, munching on the food carefully and delicately sitting on his haunches in the landing place before the door to their apartment.

All this while, Mansi remained by the door waiting for the old man lest he should need more food. When she asked him if he wanted anything more, he replied, 'No my child, I don't want anything more, but I am here to give you something!'

Surprised that the wizened old man had something to give her, Mansi asked the old man, 'Yes, Babaji, what could it be that you want to give me?'

He answered, 'I would like to provide you some answers to the problems that you have been facing at home recently. Remember, one should not hold on to things that no longer belong to you. When a beloved person passes away, one should let go of such people because remembering and grieving for them too much will not let their souls rest in peace. Also, remember what I am telling you very carefully, your sister has got something that belonged to your mother. It is the little pearl ring that she wears on one of her fingers. Remove that ring and cast it away into the Yamuna River. The ring is what connects her to her mother's soul. Your mother had given her that ring before she died.' The ascetic went away after saying these words.

These were rather strange things and Mansi wondered whether she should tell the rest about this strange episode. The ascetic went away after giving her this rather strange information. Immediately after he had left, Mansi went to the room where her sister lay sleeping. She removed the bedcover and lo, there on Rekha's left hand, on the ring finger was that silver ring with the pearl that her mother had once worn. It looked strange to see the familiar ring on her sister's left hand ring finger! Mansi however did not do anything, and she quietly withdrew from the room after covering her sister's body back with the bed cover. Later in the day when her father returned from work, she gathered both her grandparents and her father and told them about the ascetic and how she had indeed found the ring on her sister's finger. They were amazed by her story and her father went to the room where his younger daughter lay on the bed, and to his utter surprise he saw indeed the ring with the pearl that he had once gifted to his wife on a many years ago! That night, before giving Rekha her dinner, Vineet told his mother to slip off the ring from her granddaughter's finger. Not surprisingly, this was done while she was still in deep sleep. Rekha's ring finger had grown so thin that her grandmother had found it easy to slip off the ring, although Rekha had stirred in her sleep.

Vineet looked at the ring as his mind was flooded with old memories of the ride to Connaught Place, window-shopping, and then landing up inside a jewellery store. At the jewellery store, he seen this ring and had decided to gift it to his wife although she had protested that she did not want it. Amazingly, the ring fit her finger snugly; it was as if it had been made for her! After gifting her the ring, (oh it had looked so nice on her finger) they had gone to the Maharaja restaurant in Janpath and had had a lunch of idly-sambhar and *masala-dosa*.

Wrapping the ring in a tissue, after looking at it for some time, Vineet placed it on the dressing table in his bedroom. The next morning he woke up early in the morning at about five, grabbed the ring and drove on to the bridge over the Yamuna River. He stopped his car and then opening the tissue, he gazed at the ring one last time. Tears flooded his eyes, he wanted to keep the ring, a keepsake that would remind him of his wife whom he had loved so much, but then he was resolute about what was to be done. He folded the tissue back over the ring and whispering, 'Good bye Shalini!' he flung the ring over the railing into the Yamuna River. The ring along with the tissue sank into the water without making a ripple. Wiping the tears from his eyes, he drove back home.

There was somehow a marked change in Rekha after they had taken away her mother's ring. She woke up early in the morning the next day and the first thing she noticed was the missing ring. She queried the others about it but then they told her that it might have fallen off. She accepted this explanation without argument.

The day after Vineet had thrown the ring into the Yamuna River, the Pastor from the church, the Priest from the Gurdwara, and the Pundit from the temple came and said their prayers. By evening there was a faint glow on her face. The next day, her father took her to the psychiatrist. The report was that she was responding to the treatment. He gave her a change of medicines and they returned home to the joy of her sister and grandparents. Rekha recovered quickly and the neighbours ascribed her recovery to various factors, some said that the prayers of the priests had made a difference; others said that the Psychiatrist's treatment had made a difference, but no one mentioned the ring that was missing from Rekha's finger!

In the days that came to pass, Rekha re-joined school and made up for the lost classes. Her teachers and her classmates came to her rescue and gave her notes and helped her catch up with lost ground. When Rekha had completely recovered from her strange illness, Mansi, as advised by her father told her sister about the ring and about how she had driven the priests from their home. Things at the Sharma's household returned to normal and a year after Shalini's death, they hosted a dinner for all the people in the locality in memory of a woman who had been loved by her family members, a woman who had so loved her family that she wouldn't let go even after she had died. The flinging of the ring and perhaps the prayers of the devout priests had put Shalini's soul to sleep finally.

By now it was three in the morning and all of us were lost in our thoughts. My aunt came at that moment and told us that it was late in the night and that we should go off to sleep as the next day was Diwali and we had to wake up early. We said our good nights and went off to sleep. Few of us however were able to sleep as we thought about the amazing story that our cousin sister had recounted to us. The whole story had been narrated to her by Mansi whom she used to help in Physics and Chemistry. She had incidentally known Shalini quite well as she used to visit the Sharmas often.

The Prince and the Beggar

'This tale is about two friends who were brought together by fate, separated by circumstances and then brought together once again by chance after a number of years. The story of how they were brought together is as amazing as the story of their friendship as young boys!' - The philanthropist was talking to a class of underprivileged students in a slum that he had undertaken to help. He was Mr Andrew Martin, the famous steel magnate and he was enjoying the conversation he was having with the young ones, all students in the last their last year at the New Hampton School in Worcestershire. They were all students in the age range of sixteen to eighteen and soon they would be out of school, fending for themselves. A very few would probably join college while most would get a job, get married and have kids.

Andrew loved talking to these young men and women who belonged to less privileged families, they were students whose fees the parents could not afford, and so Andrew had stepped in with a scholarship for them. He shared a kindred feeling with them more so because he had undergone similar difficulties many years ago. Looking at the twelve boys and ten girls, he could see that they belonged to parents who did menial tasks to make both ends meet. There was a stirring deep within his heart as he saw how he had been all those years ago, hungry, wearing hand me downs, and always on the lookout for friends who could lend him their books. But then those times had passed, God had favoured him so much that he felt he had an obligation towards these men and women. Somehow sponsoring the education of such students reminded him of the times when he, like them had not been so lucky.

The students were now clamouring for him to continue. 'It was many years ago when this story took place. There were two very close friends, Andrew and Martin. They were studying in a very well-known grammar school in Northampton. Both of them belonged to very well to do families. They were studying for their O levels when tragedy struck one of them - Andrew. His father had suffered irreversible losses in business and soon things turned from bad to worse! Soon there wasn't any money left to pay his school fees. Martin's father however gladly stepped in and began to pay the fees because of the friendship that existed between his son and Andrew. Martin too pitched in without telling his father about it and helped Andrew with small sums from his ample pocket money. Andrew began wearing hand me downs from his friend. The whole year passed in this manner, and then finally the exams came upon them. Their teachers and their parents however were not very anxious about the two boys' result because both of them had been exceptionally hardworking, intelligent and talented students. It was not surprising therefore, that when the results came they had both passed their 'O' levels with distinction. Andrew got a scholarship from Cambridge to pursue Business Administration, while Martin's father insisted that his son should pursue the same course from Harvard. Both the boys spent the days before joining college hanging out with the girls, visiting pubs, and just roaming around the town. They drank beer and sang popular pop numbers, and did window shopping. Martin bought a few things but Andrew had little money so he just satisfied himself merely by looking at the things in the display-windows of the shops, disguising his longings for the goods with a smile and a shaking of the head when Andrew asked him if he fancied anything.

Andrew paused looking at the students - this was something special he wanted the gathered boys and girls to pay attention to what he was sharing with them - it was a story from the past, his own story and he did not want to rush it lest they should miss the message. The students became immediately aware that what he was telling them was important, and they waited with baited breath for him to continue.

'A week before they were to part, Andrew asked Martin if he could lend him a hundred pounds to see him through the first couple of months at Cambridge - he told him that he would return the money as soon as possible, and that he would look for a part time job, probably as a bartender. Martin agreed, and told him that he would give him the money the following day. In the meantime Martin suggested that they visit their favourite pub for a pint of beer, to which Andrew acquiesced. That evening, they drank beer and when they were drunk they stepped out and walked the streets singing loudly even though they were told to quieten down by the police men doing the rounds. They finally parted the best of friends, each proceeding to his home.'

The next day came and went, and Martin did not come to their fixed rendezvous, the St. Anthony Church on Beagle Street. Andrew called Martin on his mobile, the bell rang but he did not answer his call. He wondered if Martin had suddenly had second thoughts about giving him a hundred pounds, but then he dismissed the thought as being highly improbable!'

There was another pause and the students were quiet - they did not say a thing. Andrew looked at the inquisitive faces and then went on with his narrative:

'He waited for a whole week and then came to know from other friends that Martin had flown to America. Andrew was devastated. He knew that he needed a hundred pounds and that the scholarship was not enough to get him through. Resigned to his fate, Andrew joined a local garage as an apprentice mechanic. He believed that joining college would neither help him nor his family. By now his father was bedridden having suffered a stroke. His mother decided to work as an office assistant in one of the real estate firms in Northampton. Andrew finally accepted the fact that it would be better for him not to join college as his family was not in a position to afford the fees. Andrew gave up the idea of going to college and instead joined a car garage as an apprentice mechanic. A couple of years went by when the unexpected happened. Andrew was walking back home when a Bentley stopped by him. He felt embarrassed as he was wearing a worn out pair of jeans and leather jacket that had turned greasy and wondered why the car had stopped next to him, what would the passenger want with him, could it be that the driver of the car wanted to ask him for directions? His train of thoughts was interrupted when instead of asking for directions, from within the car, the passenger door opened and out stepped a gaunt man struggling to stand straight. 'Andrew, it is me Martin,' said the man."

'Martin, is that you?' Andrew asked him with amazement, for the man looked too old to be Martin his old friend, and in any case, one did not age in a period of two years, at least not so drastically? But lest his friend be offended by his inquisitiveness added quickly, 'Whatever happened to you?'

'It is a long story, Andrew,' Martin replied. 'Why don't you sit with me!' Martin replied gesturing towards the open door.

'Unable to resist the offer, Andrew agreed.' The philanthropist continued his narrative, 'The drive to Andrew's humble lodgings took a good ten minutes and on the way Martin told him that he was dying of cancer. Andrew was too shocked to reply and listened quietly to what his old friend had to say.'

'I am sorry that I didn't give you the hundred pounds that I had promised. I agree that I should have understood how important those hundred would have been to you, yes, I also confess that I had been too insensitive and selfish to stick to my promise. Anyway, I proceeded to America without giving you the money! At Harvard I managed to do very well the first year, but then it was in the second year, last year, that I began to have frequent spells of dizziness. When I visited the doctors they prescribed various tests. Of course when the results came, they had all diagnosed cancer. Andrew, I want to tell you that I have cancer, I have at the most I have a couple of months to live – and I am sorry for not meeting you before leaving for Harvard, please forgive me!'

'Andrew was astounded by what he had heard and exclaimed, 'Oh God, No!' It transpired later on that Martin, his best friend wanted to atone for the lapse that he had committed towards his friend. On the way back home, he told him that he wanted Andrew to join Cambridge once again and complete his course. Andrew protested that it was too late and that he had dropped the idea of going to college; he also wanted to accuse his best friend of having ditched him in his time of need, except that something stopped him from saying anything more.'

The students were now hanging on to his and they were curious about how the story would end, although they were all aware about how it would end; they begged him to continue with the story.

'Martin died after a week, and Andrew was devastated!' said the gentleman to the young listeners who were by now fully hooked. 'He attended his best friend's funeral till the end and when everyone was leaving, Mr Finch, Martin's father stopped Andrew because he wanted to have a word with him.'

He began as soon as he had his attention, 'Martin asked me to hand over this letter to you before he left for the hospital the final time,' he said, handing him a white envelope on which were inscribed in Martin's flowing hand, 'For my best friend, Andrew.' Underneath the first line was another which read, 'I hope you do understand!'

Andrew read the letter after reaching home. It read:

'Dear Andrew,

I want to explain to you why I left for America without contacting you. I had promised to give you a hundred pounds but unfortunately lost all the money after meeting a woman for a one night stand! The day I was to have met you, I came across a woman who seemed to be the most gorgeous women I had ever seen. She was standing at the Grand Mall main parking lot. I had spent all my money by then and the only money I had was the hundred pound bill in my wallet. Thinking perhaps that I could flirt with her a bit since she had been giving me the looks, I approached her. One thing led to another and then after about half an hour of flirting we ended up at her flat. What happened next passed off as if in a dream, a dream of pleasure mixed with regret, pain and a sense of being haunted by the devil himself. Yes, she had passed on to me a disease much worse than clap, she had passed on to me a virulent form of a cancer that spreads throughout the body like wildfire. To make matters worse, just while in the middle of doing our thing, the door burst open and three men burst indoors and beat her up before my eyes demanding how much money she had earned. When she refused to answer them, they turned their attention towards me and demanded that I should hand over to them a hundred pounds. My heart sank and before I could protest, they took out my wallet and extracted the money. They slapped me and punched me in the face before leaving us! I just did not have the courage to meet you after that, I felt guilty for not meeting you at the appointed time. I went home and told everyone that I had had a fight with some people on the street. Soon the bruises turned an ugly purple and weighed down by the shame of what I had done and not knowing how to face you, I left for Harvard with a guilty conscience as big as a truck! Life in Harvard was tough, I could not make friends and soon I began to suffer from some kind of an ailment that left me debilitated and weak. Soon it became so bad that I had to seek medical attention. The doctors told me that I had contracted a rare kind of cancer that was passed through promiscuity! I had been barely in Harvard for a year and a half when my condition became so bad that I had to return to England. I planned to make amends with you and say that I was sorry for having broken a friendship for a hundred pounds. I hoped to meet you and tell you how sorry I was. The day I met you I felt sorry to see you in that grubby pair of jeans and decided then and there to leave you some money for your upkeep at Cambridge. When I returned home, I told my father everything and he was really saddened by what I had told him. I then convinced him that the only way I could make amends to you would be to set aside a small amount of money an annuity to pay your college fee and become a successful careerist. Andrew, I request you to take the money and study in Cambridge for my sake. I am sorry for the hurt I have caused to you, please forgive me so that my soul may rest in peace! Your acceptance of this amount will give me great peace!

With lots of love
Your friend
Martin'

'Enclosed in the envelope was a cheque for two thousand pounds, a fortune that would tide him through studies and pay for more besides.'

The students were silent after their benefactor had completed reading from a few sheets of handwritten paper, the remains of the letter that Martin had left him. After a pause, the middle aged man continued, 'Andrew read the letter and then felt equally sorry about how the two friends had drifted apart. In the times to come, he relented and accepted the monetary gift that his friend had left him. He went to Cambridge and graduated with distinction. Thereafter there was no turning back for him. Corporate companies vied with each other to higher him. He joined a well-known Multinational company, served as the company head in various countries, and then after serving the company, which incidentally dealt in steel, resigned and set up his own company. Gradually, the years he became a well-known steel magnate. The man standing before you is the other man in the story, Andrew. This is the story of my life, the story of two friends!' There was a united gasp of surprise amongst the boys and girls alike when they realised that the gentleman standing before them was none other than Andrew. 'Even in moments of achievement, I don't forget that my friend Martin was instrumental in helping me achieve the position that I have today. A good friend is one who realises his mistakes well in time, and he is someone you can depend upon in the end. Martin was a good man, it is just that he made a mistake as a young man, but then he surely suffered a lot for it!'

The Man Who Went Ahead in Time

His name was Vikram Chandra, and he was selected to travel in time, the first time traveller; a voluntary human Guinea pig who had offered himself for the experiment. Described in simple words, the experiment entailed a process of breaking down an object, living or not, into digits that could be beamed into the desired time zone. The scientists called the process, 'encoding'. At the destination the digits would be 'decoded' and then converted into organic form using the organic converter. It was all very hush hush at the establishment in New Delhi, the Institute where the time travel experiments were taking place was named The C.V.Raman Institute of Fundamental Research, after the famous Indian scientist. The scientists who were doing research work at the institute knew that they were a privileged lot, and they were under the great responsibility of furthering the welfare of mankind. Most of the projects being undertaken were top secret because no one wanted the details of the projects to fall into the wrong hands! Moreover, the doomsday gurus who had begun preaching about the 'big wave' that would come out of the blue and drown them all, an assumption that global warming would result in excessive flooding resulting from the melting polar ice caps and consequent rising of sea levels. The workforce of scientists at the C.V.Raman belonged to various countries, and they were working furiously to beat the fast approaching deadline. They were scientists from twelve countries, including, the

United States, United Kingdom, China, France, Russia, Ethiopia, South Africa, Japan, Netherlands, Switzerland and a few others.

The day Vikram Chandra was to be digitised and beamed into the future turned out to be an ordinary day like others. The streets and roads were jam-packed with vehicles, The Yamuna River was flooded, the television channels replayed the week's old images of a rebel stronghold in Iraq being overwhelmed not by Government forces, but by a flash flood caused by incessant rains. The place where the camp had once been was now a lake! Global warming had made its presence felt throughout the world. Tuvalu, Kiribas, and Kivalini had all sunk beneath the advancing waves. Global warming had brought with it not just a shifting of seasons, but also rainfall in unexpected regions. The deserts were quickly becoming wetlands, while regions that had once received enough rainfall were themselves becoming deserts.

Vikram had woken up that day as usual, at five in the morning. After a warmup session he took his bicycle and rode all the way from his house in Civil Lines to Rajghat and then back. At Kashmiri Gate he met the rest of the biking gang members and they all rode together. That day however, Vikram was lost in his thoughts, he was apprehensive about the things that might go wrong. In its initial stage the time travel experiments were performed on rats, and sometimes, when the calibration went wrong, the transducer reassembled the rats' bodies in a bizarre manner, head on the back, legs in place of the mouth, and ears inside the stomach. These monstrosities managed to survive for a few minutes before dying what was probably a painful death! There were other, more horrifying instances that impacted the subjects on which the time travel experiments were conducted, but he did not want to think about them. Vikram was startled out of his thoughts by the voice Shalini, speaking to him. She was the M.D. of a multinational bank and was riding by his side.

'Is everything OK, Vikram?'

'Sorry, I was planning my day out!' he replied quickly tuning out his thoughts.

'Well, put your thoughts away, Vikram, and enjoy the ride while we still have the road, soon the Yamuna will burst over the banks and this road will soon be gone!' She exclaimed, as she burst into speed, leaving him behind.

Vikram, however could not break out of the feeling of fear that had taken hold of him that morning. He had thought about calling in sick, and he knew that Andrew Spencer from MIT, would gladly replace him, but then he wondered if he would ever be able to live with the guilt of having let down his friends. He was once again startled, this time by the loud sound of a mighty wave of water crashing over the embankment. The road was suddenly flooded with water, and the swift flow threatened to topple his bicycle. He was frightened to see that the others had already gained a healthy lead over him. Spurred by the fear of being left behind, Vikram switched to a lower gear and Pedalled with all his might making up the gap.

When he had reached the straggler in the group, Arun - an automobile spare parts manufacturer, he asked him, 'what was that sound?'

'It was the sound of a big wave crashing over the embankment!' Vikram responded.

On reaching home after an hour, Vikram had a quick shower, and then breakfast was served by his mother, Mrs Sushila Chandra. His father, Mr Sumit Chandra, a senior engineer, was fast asleep; he had been awake all night, supervising the reinforcing of the walls that kept the waters of the Yamuna from flowing in. Vikram's sister, Seema, a doctor at one of the Government hospitals in Delhi, was on night duty. Somehow, his mind was not on the breakfast that his mother had put on the table. Even after much coaxing by his mother, he barely nibbled through two *paranthas* and a glass of milk before his cab arrived for him. Waving a hasty good bye, he grabbed hold of his laptop bag and rushed out before his mother could see the tears in his eyes! Vikram knew very well about the risks involved in the experiment meant that there was a fifty per cent chance of his being able to get through!

There were a hundred different things that could go wrong - faulty decoding and encoding could result in a painful death for the time traveller, in some cases this could also result in body parts being located in the wrong place! They had experimented on flies, lizards and cockroaches, not on larger animals because of a prominent animal rights activist who was also a minister in the union government. When things went wrong the insects and the lizards became a mishmash of organic matter. As far as he was concerned, there was also a possibility, the scientists warned; that the world he was projected might be totally inhospitable what with global warming turning the whole world into a water world with no dry land to step on to!

On most occasions when things went right, the insects and lizards were perfectly OK! So far the scientists at the C.V.Raman institute had been only been able to project the subject into the future and then back again. They had also been able to calibrate the power of the beam into hours, years and decades. Vikram would be projected to 2030, a decade ahead of his own time. For this experiment, apart from his clothes, he would be carrying no metal instruments, since the experiment at present worked on organic materials.

When Vikram reached his place of work, there was a hushed atmosphere of excitement mixed with apprehension at the institute. Last minute instructions were given to him by Mr Erich Koestler, famed climatologist about climate cues and signs to look for, while Dr Hemlata Kochar counselled him about possible physiological side effects of time travel. A separate pouch of medicine would be sent along with him. Finally Vikram was made to lie on the transporter couch and put to sleep!

* * *

The projection deposited him in the town of Srinagar deep in the mountains of Uttarakhand. Strangely enough he saw lines of people marching downwards towards the plains. It was raining heavily and the mountains were awash with sheets of water. He was surprised why the people were rushing to the plains when they should in fact be heading for higher ground. It soon became clear to Vikram however that the mountains had become treacherous, with rushing streams of water threatening to cut off the roads and destroy bridges. Soon he joined a family, the Sharmas from Chandigarh who were trying to get back home. Mr Mohit Sharma was accompanied by his wife, Reema, son, Rohit, a twenty-two year old engineering student from IIT Roorkey, and Hema, an eighteen year old student of humanities from the University of Delhi. They had all come to the mountains for a change in spite of the warnings they had received from friends and relatives alike about not going to the mountains becoming treacherous during heavy rains.

Presently, strategically placed walls had managed to hold back the rushing waters of the Mandakini, Alaknanda and Ganga in some places. The scientists and engineers had managed to hold back the flooded rivers from inundating the cities and towns running down the mountains down to the plains, all the way to Kanyakumari! Vikram had learned from the Sharmas that the walls that things were safe enough in the mountains, that is until the walls themselves had started failing. Things had turned for the worse only the previous year according to Rohit.

'So then, why did you decide to come to the mountains?' Vikram repeated his question to Mr Sharma, a clerk working for the Municipal Committee of Delhi.

'We came to the mountains to pay obeisance to the Holy Shrines. After the pilgrimage to the four great temples we landed up in the town of Srinagar in order to catch a bus back to Delhi' Mr Sharma replied.

'Well here we are now!' Said Vikram, 'stuck together while it rains.'

The Sharmas along with Vikram were able to hitch a ride on one of the buses still running, but then when they reached the hamlet called Jayalgarh, they were forced to continue the journey to Rishikesh on foot. On the way down to Rishikesh they came across abandoned towns. The shutters of all the shops had been downed, the few eating joints that were still open sold food and beverages at an exorbitant rate. The samosas were stale and the tea weak, made of recycled tea leaves, but then the Sharmas and Vikram had to have something warm to fill their empty stomachs. While walking down the town with a strange name, the group comprising of the Sharmas, Vikram and a young girl of twenty-five, an adventure sports guide, Sumit, moved down the deserted lanes. They came across a number of hungry stray dogs that growled at the group. Vikram suggested that they carry sticks as a weapon against the marauding dogs. They soon came across a deserted fruit stall where there were bamboo stakes, these they carried with them. Soon they reached a town called Jagraon. It was wet all over, the incessant rain sought to soak them through their ponchos, and they were cold and miserable. However, the group plodded on. On the way they came across stranded men, women and children. They had been abandoned by the bus driver who had first promised to take them to Rishikesh but then dropped them in that abandoned hamlet saying the roads were too treacherous to drive on. Vikram exhorted the people to join them, and they agreed swelling the numbers to twenty.

All this time Vikram was wondering how he had landed in the mountains of Uttarakhand, it was clear that there had been a glitch in the transporter beam, although it had managed to transport him to the correct time zone, it had however deposited him in the wrong geographical zone! In spite of the glitch he continued to take copious notes of everything he saw so that he would have something to report to the scientists if at all they managed to retrieve him.

Finally the group reached a bridge that was almost submerged by the violently flowing waters of the Ganga. The bridge shook and vibrated alarmingly. Vikram looked at the swiftly flowing waters and shuddered to think of what might happen should they be on the bridge when it collapsed. The fear of being stranded on the wrong side should the bridge happen to collapse spurred them on to the other end of the bridge. The team of stragglers reached the safety of the other end. Soon they crossed Rishikesh and from there they could see the waters of the swollen river emptying into the flood plains!

It was at exactly at this moment that the call back mechanism of the time machine kicked in and Vikram was pulled back to the research centre! Vikram's fellow scientists welcomed him back and then he was taken for a debriefing session by the director of the institute. The descriptions provided by Vikram were duly recorded and scientists from all over the world began to calculate and formulate steps to arrest the impact of global warming. They had thought that the mountains would provide a refuge to those fleeing flooding in the plains, but now it was clear that even the mountains would not be safe. Soon, scientists, world leaders and policy-makers drafted a plan to arrest global warming. In a year or two, the vagaries of climate change were reversed and soon it became clear that the horrifying spectacle that Vikram had seen would not after take place because, finally the people that mattered had realised that they had a responsibility towards the whole world!

Vikram had become the first man to have looked ahead into the future. The experiment for time travel was discontinued for being too dangerous. In the years to come, governments across the world had managed to arrest global warming. The greatest discovery, probably of all times was that scientists at the Max Planck institute in Germany had discovered ways for converting the carbon dioxide in the air into a hard material that could replace actual wood. In days to come, industries all over the world would begin using atmospheric carbon dioxide to produce substitutes for wood, paper and even fabric! If petroleum was one of the greatest discoveries of the 19th Century, then Carbon dioxide was probably the greatest discovery of the 21st Century joked leaders all over the world!

Gone into hiding

It was a tableau from everyday life, a young man leading an older man who was bent double as if in defeat; both of them, to all appearances, tramps trudging the dusty paths of life. The summers in Jimma could be really warm, and humid because of its closeness to the Tibian Sea - a mere one hundred furlongs from the town of Kraken, that the two were crossing through. The numerous soldiers belonging to the Jimman revolutionary army barely glanced at the two men, and if any one did so, it was to turn away in disgust because they imagined the stink that came from the tramps' unwashed clothes; they thought they could also see crawling lice and other parasites in their hair, body and clothes. What the others did not notice was the tenderness with which the younger man treated his elder companion.

After they crossed the town square, they came on to the road leading to the town of Pala, a bigger town in the Trabonian province, about three hundred furlongs towards the East. There was a slight rise on their way and it caused the older man to tire badly. It was just when they hit the Pallan road that the older man simply collapsed right on a pile of garbage and animal refuse.

Immediately the younger man whispered, 'Try to get up father, I will help you up.'

'I can't, Armag, I don't think I have any more strength to carry on this journey! Just leave me by the roadside, and let me be,' his father said to him.

Armag, however did not relent, and he coaxed the older man on to his feet and led him to the stream of clear water that ran along the road. He made his father sit next to the stream and then scooped handfuls of water and washed his father's feet, hands and feet, scrubbing away at the filth that encrusted his father's clothes. There was tenderness in his actions as he tended his father with a gentleness that was an indication of the love he had for him.

* * *

The coup in the capital city Asmarina in the kingdom of Armigrage was led by the King's own cousin, Berg. It was a story of deceit and ruthlessness that bordered on malice of the most despicable kind. King Kardor was known for his philanthropy and kindness towards his subjects, so he was less interested in spending money on arms and weapons. Perhaps the greatest mistake he had committed was to hand over the control of the army to his cousin, Berg. One day, he was attacked by mercenaries, Dark fighters, hired by his cousin while he was resting in his personal chamber. He had retired to his personal chamber after conducting court. His personal body guards fought bravely but they were outnumbered by the brigands. All of his body guards were hacked to death. The King himself fought a long and valiant battle but sustained numerous wounds. It was just when he had almost collapsed with exhaustion that his son, Armag happened to step into the chamber. The crown prince, saw what was happening, and he fought valiantly, slaying the six mercenaries who had killed his father's four trusted bodyguards. Both father and son knew that they now had little time before the masters of the assassins more of them in larger numbers to investigate and finish the job. Acting with presence of mind, Armag dragged his father, the

King to the secret door that led to the tunnel dug for exactly such an event. They first entered the chamber contained the entrance to the secret tunnel hidden behind a false wall, which in turn led to a rather nondescript looking ramshackle house on the edge of the market place. Before closing the entrance to the tunnel, Armag tugged on a rope three times. The other end of the rope was attached to a bell in the King's most trusted childhood friend's house. According to a plan (that only the King, his friend Mercado, and the crown prince knew) three tugs on bell would be a signal that the King was in great danger. According to the plan set in place many years back, the King and one companion of his would be given a set of clothes fit for tramps and concealed money pouches for their secret journey to the safe house - the Marsha Villa in the town of Palla, in the kingdom of Trabonian.

Everything happened according to plan. As soon as they entered the ramshackle house, they were met by the King's childhood friend, Mercado. After a brief description about what had transpired at the palace, they quickly donned the clothes proffered by him and the money bags too. They then exited out of the house from a side door and set out on the road to the city of Pala where the safe house was located. As soon as they had left, Mercado initiated the Marjak plan. This included sending a messenger on horseback with a message to be delivered to the caretakers of the Marsha villa to secure it. The messenger also carried a slew of other instructions which were addressed to retired (yet powerful) generals, to build a force of resistance, governors were instructed to hold on to power for as long as possible.

* * *

The passage to Pala was a difficult one and the two men had to take frequent pauses. The younger of the two had to coax the elder one on. What concerned Armag the most was the fact that the injuries sustained by his father, King Kardor had weakened him so much that he feared his father wouldn't be able to make it. Finally they reached the town of Konkarn the prince had to seek the services of a medicine man. When the medicine man stripped the King to his undergarments, they were surprised to see the deep cuts that crisscrossed the older man's chest. There were places on his arms where the rebel's swords had cut so deep into the flesh that the bones were exposed! By now the King was so weak that he was delirious! The medicine man thought better than to ask about the nature of the wounds because of the amount of money that Armag had paid him. The walk from the capital city had taken them five days and they had covered a mere five hundred furlongs by the time they reached Konkarn. Armag was worried that the delay would prevent them from reaching the town of Pala on time. It took them another three days before the medicine man reluctantly allowed them to continue on their journey. They had taken lodgings in a poor man's inn and the landlord did not ask them too many questions because of the amount that he was being paid as rent.

Armag went out into the heart of the town and he became aware about what was happening in the kingdom by keeping his ears open in the public places. He overheard people say that the king's cousin had assumed full control of the kingdom and that a manhunt had been lodged to locate the whereabouts of the King. When Armag returned to their humble lodgings, he went to his father and said, 'Father, we need to move on, lest we should be caught by Uncle Berg's men!'

'Now, listen Armag,' the older man whispered. 'You should continue to Pala and manage things from the safe house. My time is almost done, and I would only slow you down.'

'No, father,' Armag replied with dismay, 'we will go to Pala, together or never!' he replied with decisiveness.

The road to Pala had been tough, and there were times when the elder man appeared to be struggling, close to exhaustion. Finally, they reached the safe house, a sprawling mansion surrounded by high walls that were almost impregnable to outsiders. Armag got his father to rest in one of the spacious bedrooms in the mansion. He was tended by a dedicated physician who visited the mansion once every day. Gradually, people who were close to the King began to trickle in, Morgot, the butler, Meanor, his nurse, and Norgan, his armourer were all there. The queen Helgard, and his younger brother Girma were still in hiding in in Asmarina. They came to know from the others that the King's close friend, Mercado, had been assassinated by the king's cousin, Berg for aiding and abetting the escape of the King.

* * *

The days passed in a dragging routine of waiting behind closed doors for more members to come. Finally one fine day, Armag received news that his uncle Berg had sent assassins to kill the King.

Armag was the only trained warrior in the safe house, and he began preparing himself for the day of reckoning when the assassins arrived. He sharpened and polished his trusted sword, Hildegard that he had hidden deep in the folds of his beggar's clothes. He gathered cleaned his two daggers and waited for the inevitable.

Finally on the thirtieth day of their stay at the Marsha villa, the first assassin finally arrived. Armag was woken by a loud noise at the gates of The Marsha villa. He leapt to his feet gathered his sword gathered his sword and rushed to the highest point on the ramparts of the walls of the villa. What he saw next amazed him to a great extent! He saw the intruder vault one of the walls which had been knocked down for repairs. In the morning light of the rising sun he saw the assassin face covered by a black cloth enter the courtyard, and make his way to the chamber where his father the King lay recuperating. Armag rushed down with due haste, challenging the intruder.

By the time Armag had reached the courtyard, the intruder had managed to fling his cloak away. In the growing light of the rising sun, he saw at once that this was no mere fighter, but rather Dark Fighter, a chimera the perfect choice when it came to assassinations and executive actions. Such assassins for hire belonged to a band of men called 'Dark Fighters'. They were a shady group of men who had no existence as real men in the world. The dark fighters had been a band of fifty who had worked under the command of his uncle Berg. During good times between the two brothers, the dark fighters had been employed in weeding insurgents from the north who had been trying to wrest control from his father. All of a sudden, the intruder took up the defensive position and withdrew his short sword from its scabbard; the rasp of steel being pulled out of the leather scabbard was like a trigger for Armag. Almost without thinking he pulled out the two throwing daggers and threw them with both hands at the intruder. One of them struck the intruded on the left foot, and he let out a loud hiss, before letting off his smoke and flash bomb. The loud report of the flash bomb stunned Armag.

By the time Armag came to his senses, no more than a few seconds later he viewed the empty courtyard and was amazed to see that the intruder had left. On looking carefully, he saw that the Dark fighter had left behind his short sword and a couple of throwing daggers. He went forward and picked the weapons left behind. They were of a strange design, and the steel was of a kind he had never seen before! He picked up the daggers and short sword rather gingerly, they felt rather cold, it was as if the metal was leaching out the warmth of his body!

He was quietly contemplating the weapons he had gathered in his hands when he was interrupted by Karl, the chief of security who followed them a few days later.

'Prince Armag, what was all that commotion all about, and what are you doing, Sir, in your sleeping robes?'

'We just had an intruder inside; he was a dark warrior, Chief!' Prince Armag replied even as he looked at the two throwing daggers he still had in his hands.

'What have you got in your hands?' Karl asked as he moved closer to the prince.

The moment he saw the daggers in his Prince's hands, Karl leaped and knocked the daggers out of his hands, 'Don't touch them Sir!' He warned the young man, 'They are made by witchcraft for assassins who are nothing but wraiths, change shapers, evil creatures who become enslaved to these weapons.'

'What, what are you saying, what happened?' Armag demanded, shaking his head as though surfacing from deep sleep, from a dream that had yet to release its hold on him.

'Trickery, Sir,' replied the guard who had been entrusted with the responsibility of protecting the King and him from assassins who were out there, searching for a moment to breach the high walls of the mansion where they had gone into hiding. 'How else would you explain the dark warrior leaving behind his weapons, that too, without a fight?'

By now, Prince Armag had recovered from the fog that had engulfed his mind, robbed him of reason and rationality, and had made him pick up the daggers and the short sword. He recalled the tingling sensation he had felt in his palms when he had picked up he daggers, the leaching of his body heat and befuddlement.

'Can you please explain, Chief?' He demanded an explanation from the wizened chief of guards.

'Prince Armag, the thing that you saw was a wraith, no human could scale the high wall of the mansion, and, you were meant to pick up the daggers. You see, the weapons used by the dark fighters are meant to suck out the vital life energy of whoever holds over a period of time. When normal human beings touch them however, the process is faster, and they in a matter of days! The Dark fighters are however immune to the effects of the dark magic in the daggers.

'I don't ascribe to such nonsense!' Armag responded, although deep in his heart he began to believe that there might be some truth in what the chief of security was saying. 'So now' he added, 'we are going to be attacked by wraiths!' He mused to himself as he turned to where the daggers lay scattered on the ground before them, gleaming with a dullness that seemed to swallow the light.

The next day they were attacked by Nazgulls, birds that had a human form with wings of huge gulls attached to their bodies. They had been prepared for the attack and had primed their bows and their arrows, Armag had with him the ten body guards who had arrived from Asmarina. The body guards, led by Karl, their officer, stepped up their volley of arrows aimed at the Nazgulls even as they swooped down towards the defenders. They were however not without casualties. First one man dropped dead, and then another, mauled to pieces by the birds that gauged and tore to bits the human flesh that they were able to reach through the unending curtain of arrows shot by the defenders of the mansion. The Nazgulls began their attack at eight in the morning and the fight went on till twelve in the afternoon. Prince Armag had fought valiantly, firing arrow after arrow at the swarm of Nazgulls that dove at them from the air. Finally they ran out of arrows, therefore they had to turn to their swords and daggers to continue their fight against the deadly birds.

Finally after the battle ended, Armag proceeded to the chamber where his father lay defeated and sick from the countless wounds that had been inflicted by the assassins sent by his cousin Berg. When he entered the chamber where his father lay, he could see that his father was in bad shape. The wounds inflicted by the men sent by his uncle's men were taking too much time to heal, he guessed that the swords that had been used by the Dark fighters were poisoned.

His father, the King saw him enter the chamber and said, 'Son what was that ruckus about?' He strained to sit up, and Armag rushed to help him sit up, placing the pillows up.

'Father, they were Nazgulls, but we drove them away!' He said with a tone of finality.

His father appeared lost in his thoughts, and then, as though remembering that his son was still standing before him responded, 'That is not the end, Armag, your uncle will send the dragons next, and you really don't have the men and weapons to fight them with!' He went on, 'It seems Berg has a very good surveillance system in place, otherwise the Nazgulls would not have found us. Tell me son, did an intruder or a wraith enter the compound a few days before the Nazgulls?'

Armag stirred with surprise and then told his father about the whole incident that had taken place when he had challenged the dark fighter.

'I touched the weapons and they were cold, as if they were leaching away my body's warmth!' He told his father.

'You should not have touched those daggers!' the king lamented, 'you were meant to touch them by our enemies, and doing so would have helped them confirm your exact location. They already suspect your presence in Marsha Villa.'

'I did not know those daggers were planted, anyway, father, I guess no harm could have come for having been contact with them for such a short time, and I would have touched those weapons for a longer time if Karl had not knocked them away.' Armag added.

'Well, what has been done cannot be undone, they know we are here,' he glanced at his son with troubled eyes, 'we will have to be very vigilant!' He concluded his statement and dropped back with exhaustion, sweat beading his brows.

Armag wondered if there might not be some other option for evading the attacks by the forces commanded by his uncle, even as he wiped at the sweat on his father's forehead. The only option it seemed was to make a break for the forest of dragon ore that was hardly fifty furlongs north of where their safe house was located. It had been about a month since they had arrived to this day, and his father had not yet recovers from his wounds. He wondered if they would be able to last even a few days in the forest! To make matters worse, it was known that the dreaded wild dogs had made the forest their home and that it was difficult to fight them off easily!

Suddenly there was a knocking at the main gate. The guards shouted loudly for the password, and promptly were provided with one. Armag rushed out of the room to the main gate in time to see a dozen of the King's most trusted troops, foot soldiers, walk in. Behind them came the Queen Helgard, his mother, his younger sister, Rebinia, and younger brother Girma. As soon as they saw each other they all rushed, embracing each other. His mother wept tears of pain and pleasure, pain for her husband, King Kardor. Girma, a strapping young man of nineteen hung back a little feeling a little awkward about the fuss that the Queen had been making. However they all recovered while the others averted their eyes not desiring to intrude into their privacy.

'Where is he, Armag?' His mother asked him in a whisper.

'There, mother,' he replied, nodding towards the chamber down the corridor where his father lay. 'Come all of you,' he nodded towards the three, 'I will lead you on,' he said even as he started to move. The Queen guided by Rebinia was the first to enter the chamber while his brother was the last.

At first it was quiet in chamber, but then soon the King stirred in his bed sensing the presence of so many people. The moment he saw it was his wife and their children, there was little that Armag could do to stop them from rushing to the bedside, smothering the King with their kisses and embraces. What touched Armag the most was to see his younger brother cast off his shyness and rushed to greet his father weeping tears of joy.

* * *

It would be about two months before the next attack would occur, but by then King Kardor recovered fully. The number of soldiers in the safe house had grown up to two hundred. Soon they would be shifting base to the Raglan fort north of Palla where they expected to be joined by twenty thousand more troops.

The attack when it came before they vacated the villa was a furtive half-hearted one and they had managed to repel the sprites and wraiths sent by

Uncle Berg. King Kardor knew very well that the final battle was yet to take place, and they would have fight back in order to regain what was theirs. In the meantime it was all about recouping regrouping and consolidating their forces.

Shadows

I wake up in the middle of the day, surprised to notice the darkness all around, the stillness overwhelms me, and then I remember the bright flash that turned the day into an inferno of blazing fires, burning everything to cinders, the heat oppressive even in the middle of the winter season! It had been as if someone had turned on a giant flash, I remember ducking back into the building, the heat searing my back, and then nothing!

'I must have lost consciousness!' I tell my other self, the one that lurks in my mind. 'That,' I tell him, 'must have been a nuclear explosion.' The news channels had been airing news about how our neighbouring country had been promising 'a special gift that would come our way.' I step out of the huge building only to be hit by the stench of burnt flesh; the heat hits me in the face. What I see shocks me a great deal, cars burnt to cinders, cars piled up on each other as if deliberately piled upon each other by a particularly angry child.

I look back towards the inviting safety of the building from which I have just stepped out, I turn around and retreat towards the building. I have just reached close to the building when all of a sudden the front facade crashes with a loud crash that shakes the very Earth, a boom that seems to reverberate in the air for ever, the sound beats into my ears like a gong that goes on and gone. I look desperately for refuge and then see the entrance to the underground shopping complex about four hundred meters on the left from where I stand. Making my mind I start walking towards the entrance. All this while I see through barely open eyelids dark objects and shapes that seem to have been men women, children, but are now lumps of coal, amorphous dark objects, one of them raises itself as if requesting for help, towards me, but even as it reaches to its normal height, it crashes into dust, a keening sound emerging from the depths of its form. I hurry on towards the entrance of the underground shopping complex not daring to look left or right but straight ahead. But even as I walk on, I sense a number of dark objects that stand up from where they are lying on the footpaths and the road; they follow me, some hobbling, some crawling, their groans and cries renting the air.

The entrance to the underground shopping complex gapes larger and larger, a huge maw towards which I am inexorably driven by the necessity of escaping from the unbearable heat, winter season turned into summer season, objects radiating heat, a tangible heat that seems to vibrate in the air, driving molecules, atoms into an agitation of anger and heat – and then I step inside, a dark cavernous space, greeted by the silence than engulfs me like a blanket a contrast to the chaos and noise outside. It is cooler the deeper I enter - nothing moves, I pass the silent counters, shop fronts that are open but unattended. As I move deeper into the space, the darkness presses on thicker and thicker, oppressive, yet comforting because it is cooler than the outside it is as if I am retreating into a cocoon a protective womb where I might rest and regain my strength. I need the security of a safe space that will somehow protect me from the conflagration and the turmoil of a burnt world outside. Suddenly I have no strength left and collapse on the ground, exhausted, willing sleep to take me into its comforting arms. I slip into a disturbed dream in which I see a thousand zombies rise up from the ground, they surround me, they reach me and then shake me, I feel myself being lifted by the shadows, I try to scream out but no sound escapes from my lips.

I wake after some time, time has suddenly no meaning for me, and puzzled by the darkness, I wonder where I am, I ask my other self, 'What has happened, why it is so dark even though it is day? Am dreaming things?' I ask my other self.

'The nukes hit the city and what you see is the aftermath,' he answers with a chuckle, 'It is dark because of the dust cloud of debris rising high into the atmosphere. The dust will remain for a minimum of six months and this can stretch to a maximum of two years. Remember it is going to be very cold because the sun will be blocked out. You probably remember the concept of a nuclear winter, don't you? Once the fires burn down, and the heat is leached away, it will become cold, very cold and then all form of life not directly affected by radiation will come to an end!'

'What about after the dust settles down, what if we can manage to hang on till then?' I ask the voice inside my head.

'By then every living thing will have died of starvation, even those that escaped the direct impact of the blast,' he says with a finality that brooks no further argument. 'Any way, there will be no vegetation left to sustain life,' he adds.

Taking the advice of the voice of my other self, I enter, what I think is a clothes shop, and grab a fleece-lined jacket that fits me, it is still warm even after a couple of days have passed since the world came to a stop. Draping the jacket around myself, I grope around, looking for a shop that has quilts and blankets, and finding one, I settle for a light blanket that I should be able to carry easily. As soon as I get what I want, I settle down in the shop on the floor and curl myself waiting for the worst.

There are ghosts all around me, I realise when I wake up. They whisper, complain, and shout at me, but I close my ears sometimes with my hands, and sometimes by humming a popular pop tune. I am surprised when the cold hits me, it has started to become unbearably cold, and I snuggle into the blanket which offers me no warmth. I now wear the fleece jacket over my sweater and body warmer, but it seems ineffective against the cold that presses on to me. It is a rather surreal experience, waking up in the dark, with no one around. The first sensation that hits me is hunger, paralysing hunger, I have not eaten for two days, and I am going crazy! I step out of the shop and proceed down the corridor, walking down a maze and lose myself. Disoriented and close to breakdown I stumble against a counter where there is still a leftover meal of two uneaten burgers and a sandwich that I dig into without any hesitation. It takes me some time to realise that they have gone bad; they stink of rot and decay. I stop, lean to one side and retch; my stomach heaves with convulsions, but nothing comes out. When I have nothing left in my stomach, better sense prevails and I grope wildly for the fridge handle. Opening the door, I pick up a couple of bottles of aerated drinks. Thankfully, I twist the cap of one of them and pour the familiar drink down my throat. I choke as the gas hits me, but carry on drinking a couple of mouthfuls and then I stop, what if I drink only liquid, I know I will have to get something to eat. I grope further into the fridge and come across a few boxes of burgers and sandwiches in sealed plastic boxes. I grab a couple and then sit on the stool by the counter to have them. My stomach growls, the moment I open the first box which contains a sandwich with sea-food filling. Not satisfied by the sandwich I open the second box and then dig into the burger.

The days pass on and finally on the fifteenth day, I step out of the underground shopping complex into a twilight zone that seems to have been taken straight out of a horror movie. What surprises me most is the caress of the snow-flakes drifting down. Pulling on the hood of my fleece jacket, I venture into the open, out into a silent world, covered in snow, the shapes rounded up by the snow, ethereal and amazing. As I walk on the main road, I am struck by the absolute silence that surrounds me, the stillness and the lack of movement hits me hard. I am on one of the busiest roads leading to the city centre called Connaught Place; it strikes me that there is no one, absolutely no one around! I walk on, in a ghost town looking at a strange buildings, I imagine gargoyles watching my progress from the tops of the buildings. I am walking in a city that is in its death throes, a ghost city, shrouded in a blanket of snow, a strange landscape where whispers have replaced the sounds of loud horns of vehicles moving around, and instead of people crossing the roads I see zombies following me. I walk on, glancing at the snow covered street light poles, trees bowed down by the weight of snow, stripped of their leaves, and then I see them, bundles of birds, pigeons, sparrows, and crows lying piled up along the roads, dogs and cats curled as if to thwart the gnawing cold. I come across people, men, women and children, some of the children still clutched in the arms of women curled around them to give them warmth, even as died, their lives leeched away, sucked away by the awful cold that now surrounds the city.

It is after sometime that I come across her, a young woman, of twenty or so, sobbing loudly, as she sits by the roadside. She has put on expensive branded clothes and I am convinced that she belongs to a well to do family. Her expensive handbag is clutched in her hands. She looks up at me as I pass, I pause and look at her face, and I am taken aback! She must have been beautiful once, but now her face has become a mess. There are blisters on her face that have turned purple-black; yellowness covers the rest of her skin. She looks at me with an imploring glance, 'Can you give me a drink, mister?,' she whimpers as she tries to stand up. I give her one of my bottles of aerated water, her hands brushing against mine, raising a shudder in me – I move on not looking at her fearing lest I should see something more horrible!. She sinks down to the ground and sighs loudly after taking a couple of sips.

The days pass in this way, my watch still works, it is an old fashioned wind up watch that my father had given me, it records the time and days accurately and I wind it faithfully. I retreat to the underground shopping complex after each foray into the city. On each trip, I come across strange sights in a town that has now become a spectre in a twilight zone, it is not dark there is enough light to find one's way through, and anyway, my eyes have adjusted to seeing in lowlight.

Nowadays I see the fires that dot the town, the fashionable woman and I are not the only people who have survived the nuclear blast, bonfires made up of remains of wooden furniture dot the city most of them are on the main roads. Rough looking men, roast the flesh of animals long dead, sinking their teeth into flesh that has long turned into bad, these are wild men, a few women too, and they seem too crazy to be trusted. I avoid them as much as possible, and when I do come upon them, I bend my head down and avoid looking into their eyes lest it should lead to a confrontation. Some of them challenge me if I draw too close to them. I flee from them fearing lest I should share the fate of animals, long dead, dogs, cats, and occasionally, a horse, a donkey and an Ox. One of the days I come across a group of men assaulting a young girl, no older than fifteen or so. They beat her up and punch her up badly - she collapses, and then they fall on her. She screams as she is overwhelmed by them, but I am helpless. She looks at me with the helpless look of one who has lost hope, our eyes meet and then she is drowned under a heaving mass of humanity as they smother her to death.

I flee from the scene, overwhelmed by a sense of guilt for not having helped her. Everything ends with a whimper and a gurgle that tells me that she has breathed her last! I am left to my own thoughts in a strange city that is on its deathbed, and I am a helpless survivor, fending for his own dear life.

Helplessness overwhelms me, I am like the shadows that flit around the city, I have no substance and yet I live. I wonder if my existence might not be like that of the zombies that I often dream about, living yet dead, feeling yet unable to change the world. I question the meaning of existence, now it has all reduced to roaming the empty streets, scavenging for food, clothes and anything that will make life survivable. I dream of another world, a world of tenderness, love, and kindness, I dream of my girlfriend and wonder what has become of her. I dream of family and friends, I dream of my boss, a strict yet kind woman. I have had no one to talk to me, except for that voice in my head, but then I want to talk to more people, not that voice that is rather too condescending and confident. He is a veritable K.I.A., a Know It All who has answers to almost everything. But I want tenderness, a soft shoulder to cry on, someone who can listen to me and not instruct me all the time.

The voice of my other self speaks to me after a long period of silence, 'You see, it all had to come to this, all that progress, all that development, every ending up in this! What you see is the result of the ultimate narrow-mindedness of men in authority, people who themselves want to impose their personal egos on the world. For such people, it is all about defending their prestige and insisting that the whole world should listen to them. They are beings who lack conscience they are without tender feelings; they have not sipped of the milk of human kindness. Social evolution has regressed to the stage where now everything depends on raw, each day that you survive adds one notch to the stick that records how successful you are in this world! The future of mankind will depend on the survival of the fittest. Hidden deep within the psyche is a beast, chained but rearing to go. This is the ultimate reality of human life, when this beast breaks the chains of reason and rationality; this is what you get – a burnt world of shadows and ghosts, a twilight world where reason and logic are replaced by the raw instinct for survival.'

'But then,' I respond to the voice in my head, 'Isn't there any kindness to be found in those that survive?' I counter that voice. 'Are we so depraved that we indulge in such destruction?' I continue asking that voice.

'You see, my dear friend,' the voice replies, 'when things comes to a head, it is all about superiority, it is all about winning the game, and as such nothing else matters except to win the game irrespective of what the outcome might be – even if it means you are the only survivor.'

The days pass, the months pass, and the cold increases. It looks as if there will be no end to the cold that has descended over the city. We are now ten in number, five men, three women and three children. We stay inside the underground shopping complex. Our days are spent in trying to keep our bodies warm, and in collecting food to feed that beast that dwells in our stomachs, we spend a lot of time in strengthening our defences to prevent the others from invading our haven. We all live in that underground shopping complex and we try to seek comfort in our togetherness; we sleep close to each other, the children in the centre, the women and men around the children in an outer circle. For all of us, our priority has become the safety of the children, one boy and two girls, all in the age group of eight to twelve. We sleep in shifts; we have rotas for defending the entrance, scrounging for food and sleeping in groups. Fights often break out between us but these are often quelled by the times in which we live. The women turn out to be the hardiest of us all even as they comfort us men and cajole us to gather food for the day. The men seem to be the most affected of all even as they break down most often; weeping about the wives and children they have left in the other parts of the city.

Everything that we do has assumed a fixed routine and we try to make the best of everything. The children strangely bind us together even as we look after them as parents. They are a source of joy and happiness in the midst of all this confusion and chaos. I miss my family, my wife and my two sons. Each one of us is lost in his or her thoughts and often we all end up weeping, wondering about how people who ordered the blast that destroyed our lives could have even have thought about launching the bombs. Is humanity so void of sensitivity, love and affection that it hardly thinks of launching weapons that bring such pain and suffering on innocent people?

We are lost in our thoughts, there are men and women separated from their families, men separated from their wives, women separated from their husbands, the children fortunately are with their mothers.

All of the people who are with me are professionals of the highest levels. They had been travelling in the metro from the airport and had alighted from the train before the blast. Every one of them has been a professional of the highest kind, in the other life. The men and women have families, wives and husbands in the other parts of the city. No one knows about the fate of the other family members. We share our fears and hopes about finding the others, but then as each day passes, our hopes fade away. The children were lucky enough to have their mothers with them.

The voice of my other self has fallen quiet, and I wonder if I am sane. I want to be with my family, and share a moment of gladness with them, but deep in my heart I fear that they have not survived the blast.

Time drags on and on, days don't end and the months drag on. The cold doesn't relent even as we go about our lives, struggling to survive. The six months pass, and the snowflakes continue to float down. Life as we know has changed as we struggle to live, cuddling together in the coldest moments, sharing tit bits and pieces of edible food as we subsist as animals driving with a need to keep warm and feed our increasingly empty stomachs. The only thing that keeps us going on is the hope that we will one day see the rays of the sun breaking though the mantle of a dark and impenetrable leaden sky, a sky that is still covered with the debris and dust of a blast that ejected a mass of living matter into the atmosphere that has clouded our lives with despair, pain and suffering!

We wait for the dawn of day to come, we are surrounded by shadows, shadows of life that might have been, shadows of people who have passed away. The shadows cling to us refusing to go away, shadows that are ghosts of a whole city. The shadows do lengthen even as the days pass by as we struggle to survive, scrounging for food and warmth that seems harder to come by. Our own lives seem to be part of a shadow that threatens to engulf our own very lives, sanity and all.

Andoran Nights

The days were spent in hiding and it was at night that the remaining residents of Andora (those who had escaped the culling) came out. It was not that the nights were safer than the days; rather it was just that the intruders were more visible at night because their eyes glowed like bright torches! It was an eerie sight the twinkling lights made up of lamps, candles, and a few solar powered lamps instead of the regular electric lights in houses far apart, it was like seeing a handful of stars in a black night. Andora had become a deserted ghost town in place of what had once been a thriving city. Why the few remaining human beings left the lights that were visible at night especially the aliens was a mystery for Sam. He, like the other remaining few had escaped the culling.

It was seven in the evening so he turned on the solar lantern in the living room of his second floor apartment. He took the precaution of never letting the light from his apartment be visible to the outside world like the fools who did so, often inviting attacks from the aliens. Soon Anton would come knocking at his door and together they would roam the streets looking for stuff to salvage.

At eight there were the characteristic three knocks that signalled Anton's arrival. Sam got up from his couch and opened the door, the chain still attached, for they had learned the hard way that you simply couldn't trust knocks at night!

'Hey, open up, it's me!' whispered Anton urgently.

'Oh, come on I am doing exactly that!' replied Sam.

Once the door was opened and Anton was admitted into the living room, Sam asked him for developments. Anton was the one who lived the farthest and his journeys were the longest, so it was but natural for him to have more information to share than the others who rarely travelled more than a kilometre from their homes.

'The D'Argent family was taken today, Sam, I didn't see any light in their living room today!' Anton began as he laid down his bag on the floor. It contained an assortment of stuff that he had carefully salvaged from Super marts, these included cans of cheese, fruits, bottles of mineral water, clothes - and yes an assortment of pistols and ammunition for the pistols.

'Why are you wasting your time on pistols?' Sam asked his friend rather irritated, for firearms had proved to be ineffective when used on the aliens - what was the point, anyway if you could not see them?

'Couldn't resist the temptation of holding a Glock or a Beretta, Sam,' Anton replied as he began to caress the Beretta.

Disgusted by this misplaced display of emotions for a gun, Sam said, 'Put that away, Anton, what is the plan for today?'

'Why not go visiting Tanya?' – Anton replied with a mischievous smile.

Tanya was Sam's girlfriend. Fiercely independent, she had refused to shift in with Sam, and she lived alone in an apartment complex in the middle of the city. A racing car enthusiast, a women's car rally champion, she had driven an assortment of racing cars, that were street legal while cars still ran on the roads, but then, all that came to an end when the aliens had landed in their city hunting human beings ruthlessly and then killing them. Tanya enjoyed playing games with the intruders, she enticed them to get her led them on a chase to where her car was waiting with the engine idling and the window rolled down to facilitate entry in an emergency and as a failsafe in case the doors auto locked. She would shower them with the choicest of invectives, in order draw them towards her. The aliens could never hope to catch her while they were on their feet; the aliens drove bulky rocket scooters that were so fast that cutting tight corners was a difficult task for them. Sam had remonstrated with her time and again and had told her not to play such games with the intruders, but then Tanya was an adrenaline junkie who lived life by the seat of her pants. Nothing less would do for her.

The reader might be wondering about the provenance of the alien intruders, well they were space-farers, aliens who had come from another planet in another galaxy. What distinguished them from human beings aside from the fact that they had intelligence was that they were more destructive, rapacious and violent than their human hosts! They were uncanny predators, no, not like the predators in that famous movie, but then yes, they were invisible, and their eyes glowed at night. Yes, they must have been heavy too because when a victim was pursued by these creatures, the only inkling he or she had was the sound of their feet slapping against the ground – that is if they were feet and not paddles!

Anton and Sam left for Tanya's place in the centre of the town riding their all-terrain bicycles, they were quiet and the only sound that could be heard was the sound of the tyres hissing on the now abandoned roads. They shifted to a higher gear and cruised at a respectable twenty kilometres an hour. The streets and the roads bore a deserted look though the empty shop front windows could hide some unpleasant surprises behind them. It was spooky, eerie, and somehow it felt as if they were being watched by eyes. But then whose eyes were they? Sam indicated to Anton that he was signalling Tanya on his walkie-talkie and then single handed pecked on the buttons on the radio that was clipped to the bicycle's handle-bar. He clicked the button on and off three times - the pre-assigned signal that they were coming in. Sam immediately got the response, in the affirmative, which meant that the coast was clear and that the wood and steel reinforced shutter to the garage to Tanya's apartment would lift to give them entry the moment they reached it, and then it would drop down sealing off the apartment from the outside world.

Everything happened exactly as planned, the shutter lifted and they slipped in just as the shutter came sliding down. 'Yippee' – shouted Anton as he scooted around, sliding his feet on the ground.

'Shut up Anton!' responded Sam - 'do you have to make all that noise?' exclaimed Sam as he came to a more dignified stop.

'Welcome young boys!' said a young woman of twenty, dressed in a pair of jeans a tee shirt, and running shoes looking at them from a doorway that had earlier not been there.

'Hi, Tanya!'- Sam called out.

'Hello, Ghost Rider! Hope you are not going out today?' queried Anton.

'Of course she is, can't you see that look in her eyes, looks like it is another of her wild moments!'-responded Sam with conviction, after all he knew Tanya like the back of his hands.

'Oh come on boys, you know today's a Wednesday and today, we will visit the Westgate Mall. We take different paths; I will drive on to the Mall's basement in the Fiat Punto while you two manage on foot.' – She told them.

'Fine there should be no problems, we leave our cycles here and then once we have gained entry into the mall, we will collect all the stuff from the shelves, put them in the bags, and then wait for you in the basement,' said Sam.

'All right, let's go, we have all the lists and the walkie-talkies are on and synced,' agreed Anton.

This was incidentally their weekly shopping trip to the Malls that dotted Andora. They never visited the same Mall twice in a fortnight, making it a point to make their trips as random as possible. Anyway, both Sam and Anton made it to the Westgate Mall well in time. Entry was affected through the service door at the back of the Mall with a set of skeleton keys that Anton and Sam carried with them. Tanya in the meantime arrived at the underground basement in the mall.

She switched off the engine and the silence in the basement was complete. According to plan, Tanya would not leave the car come what may. That way, in case anything happened to both Sam and Anton, she would be able to make a quick getaway in the car. It was a well-rehearsed plan and it had worked well till now. She would wait for the two men for an hour and then leave with or without them.

Things happened almost according to plan - both Sam and Anton went through the shelves, collected canned foodstuff, toiletries, batteries, medicines, a new set of clothes and whatever caught their eyes as necessary and important. After they had gathered all their stuff, they bundled everything into the cloth bags that they carried with them. It was only after they were done and had started proceeding towards the basement that both men sensed that they were being stalked. There was this eerie sensation at the back of their necks. Both Sam and Anton looked at each other and nodded towards each other and the exit.

'Let's get moving, I guess, the intruders have discovered us this time!' whispered Sam to Anton.

'Careful does it, just walk quietly as if you are not aware about our pursuers, and then the moment we are through the doorway into the upper basement, just run!' suggested Anton.

They both proceeded quietly towards the swinging doors leading to the upper basement parking lot where Tanya was waiting for them. The moment they were through the doors, they both ran like mad straight to where Tanya was waiting for them. They threw caution to the winds, and screamed, 'Tanya pop the boot!' as they ran for their lives. The car was still a good hundred yards away when the swinging doors crashed open behind them. Sam and Anton didn't dare turn around and they just ran on to where the Fiat was idling. Tanya had popped open the lid of the boot and now she could see the two men running towards her. She quickly unlatched the passenger doors and the rear door on her side, giving the accelerator a slight blip. Anton managed to fling himself into the rear seat dragging the bag of stuff with him, while Sam threw the bag into the boot and he had barely had swung the lid down when the car started to move! He somehow gulped an irrational fear that his girlfriend was leaving him to be eaten by the alien intruders – and ran towards the still open passenger side door in the front. He couldn't help looking back, and there just a few yards away, perhaps eight yards away were the tell-tale yellow glowing eyes of their pursuers. Somehow Sam managed an extra burst of energy and leaped into the front passenger seat as Tanya gunned the Punto's engine shooting up the curving ramp. She was a mad woman when she drove; both men had accepted this as a fact. The tyres screeched on the concrete spinning and skidding bellowing a thick cloud of smoke, they could smell burning rubber, and then they were off as the car leaped towards the curving walls of the passage. The glowing eyes of the aliens could be seen through the smoke, and surely they were too close. Tanya looked into the rear-view mirror one last time, she could see that the monsters had almost reached the car; she floored the accelerator one last time and concentrated on the exit that loomed ahead. Just when both Sam and Anton felt they were going to crash into the walls of the passage, the car shot out into the main road, leaving the predators behind them although still in hot pursuit. The glowing eyes pursued them for a good half a kilometre before letting go.

Later, as they sat at the dining table at Tanya's flat eating their *seekh-kebabs* and *shahi-paneer,* they discussed their narrow escape from the predators.

'I thought you were going to crash into the curving walls of the passage leading to the exit, murmured Anton.

'Anton, I knew what I was doing!'-snapped Tanya. She didn't tolerate any kind of criticism about her style of driving ad they knew better than to argue with her.

'It seems the intruders were waiting for us on the top floor, in the women's section of the Mall,' said Sam, 'It looks like we need to change our plans. Aliens are on to us!' he added.

'We need to change our timings and modus operandi,' Tanya agreed and then changing the topic she went on, 'Why don't you stay at my place today? I know, I was able to shake our pursuers down the road, but then you don't know the intruders might be prowling the streets close to here looking for us.'

'I guess that is what we ought to do,' Sam agreed and Anton nodded his head in assent.

Little did the trio realise that the intruders had been indeed, prowling the streets looking for them. The intruders did not know that they were all gathered at Tanya's flat. After prowling for a good three hours, the intruders finally left at about four in the morning convinced that the trio were not there. All this happened while the three slept fitfully in the living room of Tanya's flat. Tomorrow would be yet another day of struggle, a battle of wits between the survivors of Andora and the intruders that had come to kill them all and take over their city.

Note: An earlier version of this story figures in my Novel, The Other Side of Love, Beyond a Shadow of Doubt in the 16th chapter with Rohit telling his girlfriend Neena this story.

A Ghost Story

He was in deep sleep when he felt someone shaking his bed. Waking up with a start he realised that it was quite dark and the glow of the night lamp barely managed to illuminate the room. Tom did not believe in ghosts or even supernatural phenomenon, although his relatives had told him that there was a woman in the neighbourhood, a woman in white who walked on top of the buildings at night. She started her journey from the neighbouring building adjacent to the one in which he was sleeping and then would walk on to the next one before flitting on to the one where he was sleeping that night.

Tom was pursuing his B.A. (Hons) English course from one of the colleges in Delhi and had come to Gurgaon to spend the night at his grandmother's house because she had gone to visit her son, his uncle in Jodhpur. He had agreed reluctantly to his grandmother's wishes because he had planned to take his girlfriend to a movie at the PVR in Saket, but then of course, you had to listen to your grandmother after all! It was for one night and that too a Saturday, his grandmother would be back the next day. Groaning with disgust, he turned to his mobile phone to check the time and realised with a shock that it was twelve midnight, not that it affected him in any case for he was not superstitious, nor did he believe in ghosts after all!

Even as he lay on the bed, unable to sleep, he remembered how Gurgaon had once been a small town which had turned into a huge city seemingly overnight with all the top corporate head offices headed to it. Realty prices had shot up and the only thing you could find were buildings and more buildings. The greenery, farmlands, and fresh water bodies had all disappeared from sight even as they were swallowed up by builders who wanted to build apartments on them. His grandmother's house a huge villa and a few others houses were the remaining homes from the sixties the rest had all been broken up and turned into commercial complexes, shopping centres, showrooms and even hospitals! Tom remembered how in earlier days all his uncles, aunts and their family members would gather at his grandmother's house and then his cousins along with him would all have a gala time playing on what had now become a two-lane road. They told each ghost stories, played hide and seek, police and thief, and even hop scotch. They had been six cousin brothers and four cousin sisters. Now most of them, elder to him of course, had settled in faraway places, a couple, even settling down in America with their families. The house that had once been noisy and overcrowded was now rather quiet and a bit lonely. He wondered how his grandmother managed to live alone - although she was visited during the day by the family members of two of her sisters who lived nearby, in spite of this it must have difficult for her looking after the house all alone. He was not however very surprised because in any case his grandmother had been a veritable iron lady who managed things on her own.

It was in the midst of all his musings that it happened, rather randomly, not something to be frightened of, an innocuous tug on his foot. Then it happened again, this time the tug was more insistent, somebody had pulled his right foot. He flung his blanket off himself and then jumped out of bed. His heart was beating hard against his chest as he fumbled for the light switch and managed in the process, to knock off the table lamp from the side table. 'Heck what the heck!' he exclaimed as he gingerly felt for the light switch.

He found it but the moment he clicked on it, it wouldn't work! 'No, no!' he shouted to himself, 'the MCB must have tripped when the lamp fell down causing the bulb to short.' He knew he was in trouble; for to fix the MCB switch, he would have to step out doors in the dark, a prospect he did not really look forward to! The door from his room opened into the sitting room and from the sitting room he would have to walk all the way to the landing place. He would have to find his way through the furniture that literally overflowed the place. His grandmother's house had literally become a dumping ground for all of his uncles' and aunts' unwanted furniture and stuff. Grumbling to himself, Tom shifted his attention towards locating the mobile phone he had left on the bed. It was just when he had turned back to the bed to look for the phone that he heard a woman calling his name!

'Tom, Tom, listen to me, why don't you just follow me, I will lead you to the MCB switch!' the woman said although he hadn't seen her as yet!

'Shit,' he exclaimed to himself as he desperately began looking for the phone, he needed light to see beyond the lurking shadows, moreover the presence of the woman in the house surprised and shocked him! He was sure he was going barmy. The more he thought of the voice, the more he began to panic, wondering where the mobile phone had gone - it had been on the bed but it wasn't there anymore! He must have flung it off the bed along with the blanket. Now he began to sweat even more although it was still the middle of the winter season. He became more frantic looking for the mobile phone and then he stepped of a fragment of glass, the remains of the bulb that had smashed when the lamp had fallen. 'Ouch!' he shouted again as he felt for his foot. His hand came off wet; the glass shard had apparently cut into his foot - his left foot. Shaking with anger and fear, Tom just collapsed on the bed and stared into the distance from where the woman's sound had come.

'Are you looking for this, Tom?' asked the voice - it was the same voice, the one that had spoken to him earlier!

He began to shake even more, but then when he looked carefully he saw his mobile phone lying on the ground, its pilot light winking in a welcoming manner he felt reassured. Taking a deep breath of relief, he moved towards it, but before he could reach it he was stopped by the woman's voice.

'You will have to listen to what I have to say, before I let you have your phone, Tom, will it be OK if you just sit on the bed calmly, without the lights and listen to me?'

'OK, fine….I guess I might as well sit down, but then what do you want from me, just let me get my mobile phone, I have already smashed up my grandmother's antique lamp and I will get a shelling from her!' He mumbled rather incoherently as he sat down rather reluctantly on the bed.

'Would you like to see me, Tom?' said the voice close to him now.

The proximity of the voice sent shivers up his spine, 'No,…no, I mean,…yes, if it's OK with you!' He replied, changing his mind lest she might be offended by his refusal.

And then he saw her mere four feet away from his bed, a woman who was in her early thirties, dressed in simple white, she was one of the most beautiful women he had ever seen. There was something serene about her face which was filled with innocence and yet, sadness! She was simply gorgeous in a way that the girls he had known were not, could never be! He had heard about her, from many people, relatives and neighbours alike, but had never known her to be so beautiful. He knew somehow, that he would have to control himself lest he should begin treating her like a real human being. Even as he thought his thoughts he felt helpless knowing very well that the woman had already bewitched him. He thought suddenly about Sonia his girlfriend the girl with whom had been madly in love and then he felt a little guilty.

'Can I sit beside you?' she continued.

'Ah... oh...yeees... OK, I mean, sure, why not?' He answered her stammering rather uncontrollably at a ghost that must have been, what like centuries old?

There was a slight shift in the mattress, as if someone was sitting down, and there she was sitting on his left side. The scent of Cinnamon and citrus wafted from her, close by he could see that she had light golden hair, and her complexion was milky white, not the colour of death, rather the colour of health with the lightest tinge of pink in it. Her dress, now that he saw it from close was white silk and muslin, rather like a marriage gown! Even as he was observing her with a complex mix of disbelief curiosity and fear, she shifted a little closer to him and put her hand on his shoulder! He shuddered involuntarily believing that it would be the touch of death, for to be touched by a ghost would mean you had lost it! To make matters worse, he had felt the tug on his toe, then he heard her voice, then he smelled her perfume, and now this touch. It was however a rather light touch - the wind caressing him, and surprisingly enough, after the initial fright, he was somehow more comfortable.

Now that she was next to him, she addressed him, 'Look, Tom, you know who I am, a ghost in your terms, but in my language, I am a spirit that has been roaming this place for ages, trying to get someone worthy enough to listen to my story and help me out. I was the wife of the British Garrison Commander, Richard Black who was based in Gurgaon from 1880 till 1905. It was towards the end of my husband's term that a great tragedy struck the family. In the year 1905 the whole country was affected by a cholera epidemic. Our two sons, Antony aged five and Jack aged three were struck by the epidemic. They fought the disease bravely but then little could be done to save them. Alas! They died of the disease – Antony on the fifth of March, and Jack on the seventh of April, a gap of barely a month. We were broken up by this tragedy, my husband and I! Richard was so broken up that he did not want an extension for his term, so when his term came to an end in the month of December, 1905, he decided that we should leave for London in a month's time. I however did not want to leave my children behind; I wanted to stay back just to be close to their graves. We fought a lot, Richard and I but then I just did not want to return to England. Finally on the day of our departure from Gurgaon I simply disappeared from the garrison. I took my horse and rode to the hamlet of Baas, where the officers went hunting for tigers and other animals. I stayed in that hamlet with the good headman and his wife for a fortnight. The soldiers came looking for me, but then I managed to hide from them. Finally after the fortnight was over, I took my horse and then rode back to Gurgaon. When I reached the Cantonment area, I was apprehensive about being caught by the soldiers so I decided to find shelter in one of the fields close to the main bazaar. Leading my horse to one of the fields, I happened to come across a well. Being thirsty, I bent down to see whether it had water or was a dry well. Somehow I tipped too far and fell into the well. There was no one around although I shouted on top of my voice! I swam in the water for as long as possible, until finally I had to let go because of exhaustion. I remember that my last thoughts were that ultimately because of my stubbornness, I had lost both of my sons and my husband!'

There was a pause in her narrative as Tom tried to assimilate what he had been told by the woman, not spirit who was sitting next to him. He now looked at her with a new sense of respect, she was not just another woman, but rather a woman who had suffered a lot, and now she regretted abandoning her husband. But still, he thought, 'She is a sprit, a ghost, and I should stay away from her as much as possible.' He remembered being told by someone in the family that 'if you heard your name being called out at night even when there was no one,' you were not supposed to respond to that name. They had been warned by some of the elders in the family that when a dear one passed away and then happened to return to anyone in a dream or vision and asked him or her to accompany him on a journey, one was supposed to refuse point blank even if it meant one was being rather too forthright!

His thoughts were brought to a standstill when the woman continued her narrative, 'No one knew that I had fallen into the well and before long, the water in the well mysteriously dried up and then debris and mud was thrown into the well to fill it up. Soon that land was sold and a house constructed on it. The well is incidentally located in the neighbour's plot adjacent to your grandmother's house. The well is close to your neighbour's kitchen in the backyard. There is a square platform over the opening of the well where your neighbour has placed a few flower pots.'

Tom broke into her narrative, 'What do you want me to do?'

'I want you to go to your neighbour and tell him about my story. After you do this, you are to go to the well, remove the slabs, (they will slide away) of course with Mr Kamal's permission and then you are to dig out at least a handful of dirt from the well. Please bury this handful of dust in the graveyard and ask your Presbyter to say a prayer for my soul.'

'But what about your name, I need to know what you are called!' Tom said to the woman, knowing well that he would have to give the Pastor a name or so.

'You never ask a spirit her name; let it suffice you to know that I might be referred to as Mrs Richard. You must also be wondering why the elders in your family have been talking about me, well for all those years I have been wandering in the neighbourhood looking for someone to get me a release from this existence, however each time I stepped out, whoever saw me would flee indoors looking for the company and safety of others. You happened to be around this night and so I thought of communicating with you, I just hope you don't mind the imposition!' she remarked gently.

'No not at all,' Tom replied with enthusiasm and confidence for now he was sure that her intentions were not bad, and anyway he wanted her to get a release from the kind of existence that she had been leading all those years.

'Your helping me out will ensure that I will be able to achieve final rest, and yes I will not haunt you people any more though God knows it was never my intention to cause anyone any kind of harm! I have known each of the members in your family having seen them for so many years. Somehow I have felt secure and comfortable when all of you used to come home to enjoy your holidays. Now however hardly anyone come here, and your grandmother is growing old. I fear things have changed, and the loneliness of sharing the space with only your grandmother and Kamal, not getting to listen to the voices of children has made me tired.'

'Don't worry, Mrs Richard, I will do as you have told me, and I am sure you will achieve peace!' Tom assured her.

The moment he gave her his assurance the woman disappeared as if she had never been there. There was, however the linger smell of her scent, Cinnamon and Citrus blended together. The next day was a Sunday and Tom did as he had been told. The pastor agreed to perform the ritual and the handful of dust from the well was buried in a hole dug in the graveyard. The private burial took place after morning mass and it was attended by his grandmother, the Presbyter and Mr Kamal, their neighbour.

Escape from Athabasca

He had fought with his wife over a small matter of how much he should pay for the new fridge, and then left home threatening never to return. Now he regretted it, but then it had become a matter of prestige for him so he continued driving on the highway towards Athabasca. The drone of the motorcycle engine and the stretching ribbon of the road, the whisper of the wind somehow spurred him on to a fate he seemed to have no control. It was a big cruiser bike, an expensive one at three thousand dollars, but then he had always wanted to buy a Norton Cruiser. Selma and he had fought over the need to buy the bike, but then rather surprisingly he found it parked in the courtyard one fine day. Selma had bought it for him!

Glancing at his watch Segan saw it was four in the morning - he had been riding the bike for close to four hours now although he had taken a bio-break one hour after leaving Selma behind at Tenacre. He had covered a good two hundred kilometres and would soon be hitting the outskirts of Athabasca. It was getting brighter with the sun approaching the horizon. It had been a soothing ride in many ways and he knew that once he reached Athabasca, he would turn back for the return journey to Tenacre. He would apologise to Selma when she returned from work at the Tenacre Institute of Mental Sciences where she taught Psychology to University students. He would probably cook a savoury dish of mixed vegetables and fried rice (her favourite) and they would be friends. His thoughts now drifted to his job. He taught Mathematics at the Rangers' High School and they were off for the week after the annual exams. He would be taking up a new class this term, grade eight besides the three sections of twelfth that he took. The school head wanted an experienced teacher to take a lower class alongside senior classes and he acquiesced knowing that it would add to his experience.

He was just ten kilometres short of Athabasca when he heard the distant sounds of trucks and helicopters headed in his direction. Segan continued driving towards Athabasca in spite of the sounds of heavy traffic heading towards him. As he got closer to the town, he was dismayed to see people fleeing towards the South, the direction from which he had come. It was clear that the trucks and the helicopters were heading north towards Athabasca. Hovering above the trucks were military helicopters that were sweeping the area ahead the trucks, reconnoitring, it seemed possible for possible obstacles on their way, or maybe any opposition that they might meet. 'Hey,' he mumbled to himself, 'I hope that is not what I think it is an invading army heading towards Athabasca!' he wondered loudly to himself. Soon it became clear that he could not proceed any further against the flow of traffic heading south wards towards Tenacre. He was headed towards the advancing cavalcade and it now seemed to be a bad idea to continue. In any case it was now too difficult to turn around and head back towards Tenacre because the road was completely clogged by a mass of humanity flowing in one direction. Kicking out the Side-Stand of the motorcycle, Segan dismounted and then accosted a decent looking man who was carrying a camera slung around his neck and a whole lot of camera equipment in a bag.

'Hi,' he addressed the man who apparently was a journalist, according to the identity card clipped to his pocket, 'I am Segan, and I have been driving towards Athabasca from Tenacre, what's going on over there?'

'Hi,' replied the other man, extending his right hand to shake Segan's hand. We have been attacked by the Tarkian army. They apparently want to use the residents of Athabasca as Guinea Pigs to test their Bio-chemical weapon,' he remarked in a matter of fact voice. 'By the way, I am Soldan Kermik, a reporter with the Western Herald News Syndicate,' he added as an introduction.

'Well,' Segan went on to introduce himself, 'I am a Maths Teacher at the Rangers' School at Tenacre, I had decided to undertake a solo ride on the express way and here I am, not a good idea, I guess!'

* * *

By now the crowd had increased ten times, and Segan could see that it would not be possible to ride his motorcycle through this crowd. He finally unlocked the lid to his side Pannier and took out his extra tee shirt, utility box and then leaving lock in the ignition, for what would it matter, he began to walk back the way he had come. Soldan had left him with the advice to avoid any kind of contact with the Tarkian army regulars. He had also told him as concisely as possible that the Tarkian scientists had developed a bio-chemical weapon, and for its delivery had managed to fill it inside a canister that contained millions of fine needles. Each needle, as fine chaff contained a bio-engineered agent; when the canister was dropped from a helicopter it would burst open, spreading the cloud of needles far and wide. The needles would then float in the air, carried by the wind till they landed on human beings and animals alike. The moment they landed on a human being, or for that effect and an animal, the needle would then burrow into the skin and then the flesh of the victim. Once in place, the needles would discharge their poison into the bloodstream paralysing the victim. The victim would then slip into a state where the limbs refused to obey the commands of the brain although the mind worked well and all sensation and perception remained acute and alert. The state of paralysis, lasting a whole day would then fade away allowing the victim to regain movement in the limbs. This would be followed by high temperature, and a wasting disease that turned the victims into raving mad, scarecrows, and zombies who would be around for a week, biting, infecting and harassing those who had not been affected by the Bio-Agent. The Bio-Chemical agent had been programmed not to affect the Tarkian soldiers.

Segan walked with the crowd back the way he had come. He remembered that he was carrying his mobile so he took out the phone called up his younger brother, Stepan, a fire-fighter at Tenacre. In as few words as possible, he explained the whole situation to him.

Stepan listened quietly to his elder brother and then said to him, 'Look Segan, you need to get to Dessie, about twenty-five kilometres from where you are. I will drive to the central plaza in the ATV and pick you up. The army has been mobilized and they will be marching towards Athabasca any time. You need to reach the town as quickly as possible; we are glued to the TV sets and know that the situation will soon turn volatile. Just get out of that place!' he urged his brother.

Segan protested that he was on foot, and would probably not be able to make it to the town of Dessie, but then his brother told him that he would have manage somehow. Before switching off his mobile phone, he told his brother to check in with Selma. He would not be able to call her on her mobile phone as he had to conserve the battery on his mobile as it was below half; he had forgotten to charge it before leaving Tenacre. After his call to his brother, Segan texted Selma, 'Sorry I fought with you; I will make up with you by preparing your favourite savoury dish of stewed vegetables and fried rice. Love you and miss you! Have talked to Stepan and told him about everything. I will be switching off my mobile to conserve the battery. Love, Segan.'

The trudge southwards had become more of a disorganised shamble and Segan could see very clearly that if they could not press on at a faster pace, the Tarkians would be upon them before noon. In desperation, Segan looked back towards the road leading to Athabasca, and he was shocked to see that the crowd had not only increased in size, but also seemed to have stopped moving at all! It looked as if it was a cork tightly wedged in the narrow mouth of a bottle. They were sitting ducks that could be picked at leisure by the Tarkians. No sooner he had entertained this thought, than there was a commotion at the back of the crowd, and a surge that pushed those in the front like a powerful ripple pushing all obstacles out of its way. He could see that the Tarkian advance scouts had reached the rear end of the mass of humanity, and they were firing at the stragglers, strangely enough they did not seem interested in taking any prisoners!

What happened next was similar to the chaos caused by an overflowing river bursting through its banks. The people started fleeing away from the highway into the fields and farms abutting the highway. Segan also took to the fields in a jog that he hoped would take him away from the attacking Tarkian soldiers. However, soon progress became difficult as his feet began to sink into the freshly ploughed earth. Ten minutes of mad rush had left him exhausted, he paused, just for a moment to regain his breath and looked back the way he had come. What he saw at that moment would remain etched in his mind for a long time – he saw what was a meticulous culling of the people who had fled from Athabasca. Men, women, old and young, were being pursued by the Tarkian soldiers, mowed down, ambushed, and chased mercilessly. Those fleeing from their pursuers screamed while the hunters bayed, shouted and hooted even as they hunted down the hapless people. It had become a mad rush for safety for the people, but there was none as each one of the fleeing men women and children were felled one by one. The Tarkians used pistols and bayonets at close quarters to mow down the fleeing mass of humanity.

Segan soon realised that he had made a mistake in pausing to take a breath and turning round to look at the Invaders he had lost a valuable start on the pursuers for soon there was a shout and he realised that his pursuers had seen him. Obeying the instructions of their officer, the soldiers split into two groups intending to trap him in a pincer like movement. Segan however had trained well, jogging and cycling in the early morning hours before going to school to teach. That training had given him an edge over his pursuers. He knew that the only way to escape from that pincer like movement of the enemy was to stay ahead of the two pincer claws, thus taking a deep breath, Segan continued running. The game could not however go on for long because, while his pursuers kept on being replaced by fresh ones dropped by helicopters, it seemed someone was taking special interest in his capture, otherwise why would they send fresh soldiers by helicopter? Soon the pursued and his pursuers had left the other people far behind. By now Segan felt truly exhausted, because he was the only one who had to run continuously. Somehow, the soldiers soon stopped pursuing him; they stopped as one and turned their heads towards the North where a huge dark cloud seemed to be forming in the sky. He knew that something worse was coming his way and managed a spurt, increasing his speed briefly until he reached what seemed to be an abandoned farm.

The moment he reached what appeared to be an abandoned farm, and throwing caution to the wind dodged into the low doorway of one of the barns and collapsed on the ground. Panting and gasping, Segan decided to face what fate had in store for him. He gathered his thoughts and wondered why had fallen back. They returned the way they had come, called back no doubt by their commanders. After what seemed to be ages, Segan stepped out of the barn cautiously and looking toward the north, where Athabasca lay, he saw to his dismay that the dark clouds he had seen in the sky far away in the North had drifted closer to where he was, and he noticed that the clouds had descended to a lower altitude! It was a matter of time before that cloud was upon him, and then there would be no escaping from the deadly agent that those clouds contained. Desperate and helpless, he began walking due south hoping that the wind would slow down the movement of the clouds in his direction. After about half an hour, he reached what appeared to be a working farm. At the farm he could see someone, a woman in her middle ages, ploughing the field with the help of a plough attached to the tractor. The farm strangely enough seemed to be devoid of anyone else.

Rushing towards the tractor he waved to the woman who immediately stopped the tractor. 'Who are you?' the woman asked him.

'I have just escaped from a bunch of Tarkian soldiers who have taken over the town of Athabasca. They have killed a lot of people, and now have unleashed a Bio-Chemical agent over the whole area. It is only a matter of time before the deadly cloud reaches us!' he gasped.

Marja, for so her name was listened to him before informing him that her husband and their two middle aged sons had gone to Dessie to visit his brother whose wife had just delivered a son. He immediately coaxed her to drive the tractor to Dessie along with him. At first she refused to budge, but then digging into his bag, he showed her a bundle of bills and told her that he would pay her two-thousand Fills. But then she was a tough one and agreed to take him to Dessie only if he paid her three-thousand Fills. Unable to argue further because of the urgent need to get away, he agreed however reluctantly. He quickly collected bottles of fresh water, and a can of diesel fuel as directed by his new acquaintance while she collected some papers, that appeared to be cash bonds and a nasty looking rifle. After locking down the barns and the farmhouse, they set upon the onward journey to Dessie – an odd couple, a young man and a middle aged woman who drove the tractor like a mad, Formula one race-circuit driver. They took the interior dust tracks which were more like cattle tracks beaten out of the undergrowth by the passage of cattle and other domesticated animals out to feed on fresh grass. Many a times they came to ditches and culverts which seemed impossible to cross, even on a tractor, but then Marja managed somehow. It was getting dark and they had been travelling for ages it seemed before they reached the outskirts of Dessie. Marja took a break during this wild rush to call up her husband before hitting the highway to the town. The drive on the highway was so smooth that Segan nearly fell asleep. Strangely enough the highway was deserted, there were no vehicles on the road and an eerie emptiness engulfed them. Finally they reached Marja's brother in law's house at eight in the night. After a brief introduction with the other family member and relatives, for they were all prepared for the trip to Tenacre in the family minibus, he took his leave of them after handing over the cash and asking them the directions to the town plaza.

There at the town plaza was the red SUV bearing the Tenacre Fire Department Licence plate. The town was emptied of its inhabitants who had apparently fled the advance of the Tarkian army. Overjoyed by the sight of the vehicle he rushed to its side to be hugged at first by his brother and then his wife Selma. Without too much delay in the form of explanations about the strange incidents that had taken place that day, they rushed towards Tenacre, the last remaining people to escape from the advancing invaders. The highway was deserted, their vehicle being the only one to be seen for miles. Segan finally slipped into deep sleep, his head cradled by Selma on the back seat.

Later he would describe the events of the day to his wife Selma, his brother and a team of journalists and defence specialists live on TV. The Tarkian army's advance had however been halted much before they had reached the town of Dessie by the combined armed forces of Tenacre, Athabasca, and Kermania. World leaders condemned the attack on Athabasca by Tarkian army, and especially the use of Bio-chemical weapons. Segan was able to reconcile himself with his wife, and yes he did make the savoury dish to be eaten with rice.

Tanya Bhojwani

Tanya Bhojwani, yes that was her name, a student of grade twelve, all of seventeen years old, a sports woman who represented her school in the National Swimming championships, and had won gold. She was both academically as well as physically inclined a fitness freak, the pride of the Global International School at Saket, Delhi who won straight As. in all her written tests. Six foot tall, beautiful as everyone averred, she had elected to play the virtual game - Driven. Her parents, teachers and boyfriend, Kartik Singh had pleaded with her not to go for the game but to no avail.

Driven was a deadly virtual game that had taken more lives than any other game so far. It had driven young people into insanity turning them into nervous wrecks with no other option than to be admitted into mental asylums. The risks were fatal if the player did make it out of the ring of fire from which very few were able to escape. Actually, what happened was that the neural interface got damaged and this led to damaged neural transmitters, damaged nerve ends resulting in loss of memory, poor psycho-motor coordination and epilepsy. The fear caused by the image of the lion face appearing each time a contestant slipped and the pain of being attacked by serpent like monsters that emanated from the ring of fire in the penultimate round left mental wrecks left and right.

The game in itself took a whole week to run and the contestant was confined in a veritable prison for this period of time in which there was no access with the outer world in any case. All the physical parameters and vital signs of the contestant were monitored and necessary medications were administered via the intravenous injections, although, these medications could do nothing to mitigate the mental trauma that was inflicted by the game. The world wanted gladiators and games that were full gore and violence, but then it was simply not possible to have live games like the Romans did in arenas.

In spite of a lot of opposition, the government kept turning a blind eye towards this virtual game. The reason for this was not known. Anyways, driven was a popular game that was telecast live on prime time TV and the TRP ratings for this reality game blew the charts.

The rewards of winning the game offset the risks that the contestants were prone to. These included a cash reward of a million dollars, a house in posh locality and a pension that would take care of the contestant as long as she or he lived. Tanya Bhojwani had decided to go for the game that would be telecast all over the country and the world because of her father who had been diagnosed with cancer and was battling for his life in one of the speciality hospitals in Delhi. The amount that she could win would hopefully go towards the exorbitant expenses entailed in the treatment.

That day she and Kartik had gone to the Talkatora Gardens and she told him that she had enrolled in the virtual game - Driven. Kartik had remonstrated with her saying, 'Why, Tanya, why are you doing this? Don't you realise that you might never come out of the game sane?'

Tanya replied, 'But then what other alternative do I have? Dad is in hospital and we don't have the means to continue his treatment! My mother who is a staff nurse in Willington hospital cannot afford the treatment!'

'But what about our relationship have, you not thought about it?' Kartik asked.

'I am sorry, but I had to get into the game because of Dad,' Tanya, responded. 'The advance amount itself is enough to pay for the treatment!'

Tanya was finally able to convince Kartik that she had had to sign the contract with the makers of Driven because she couldn't abandon her father. He realised that Tanya had a valid point and so he did not press the matter further.

That day when they returned home to Kartik's house they made love like they would never ever get another opportunity and had parted as if they would never ever meet. There were tears in Kartik's eyes as he led her to the taxi waiting on the road below his apartment. Kartik was an engineering student two years senior to her studying at IIT Roorkey and they had become friends at school when he had been in grade ten and she in grade eight and he had rescued her from a group of grade ten students who had been bullying her for being an aspiring swimming champion who had superseded Anoushka, another girl who was the favourite of the school for her looks. Since then, both of them had got into a relationship that was initially frowned upon by their parents. Now, two years since their relationship had flowered, they both knew that they were meant for each other, and their parents had accepted that both were madly in love with each other.

Day One

The task before Tanya was about killing all the monsters in the underground catacombs below a ruined building. For this game, Tanya was armed with a machine pistol and nothing else but a commando knife. These were monstrous leeches that could move at the speed of light, and amazingly, they lived underground in the soil. It was while taking a few tentative steps down the maze that she felt the ground under her feet beginning to vibrate. At first she thought it was a freight trains passing overhead, but then after sometime she realised that the vibrations continued even when they should have stopped, with the freight train having moved away. It was while she was lost in her thoughts that the ground in front of her erupted into a fountain of dust rocks and something that reared out, a giant leech that had evil looking teeth around its mouth. To make matters worse, the teeth were angled in such a way that once they grabbed hold of the victim, pulling away would only impale the hapless victim further. Just as she was standing undecided, the unthinkable happened – her feet simply gave away from under her and she simply collapsed on the ground! It was falling down on the ground probably that saved her. The leech, unable to see Tanya retreat into the hole it had made. She realised that the leeches were able to detect the vibrations made by her feet as she walked around the maze. The moment she realised what was happening, she began to walk more cautiously and softly, trying in the process, to make as little noise as possible!

It was towards the end of the game that she tripped on an obstacle on the ground and fell down once again. She believed her game was over because now she was sure that the leaches would sink their teeth into her and suck all her blood. Right then she had a glimpse of the lion face, the eyes glared at her with a malevolence that took her breath away, the eyes drilled right into her soul and she faltered. It was in that moment that she began to have doubts about whether she would ever get to win the game. Lying on a virtual ground, waiting for the monster to finish her, she thought about her options, losing her sanity and being sent to a mental asylum, losing the father she loved, losing the boyfriend she wanted to marry one day, and the mother who would wail the silent tears of a woman torn in grief, but no, she couldn't back out, so she rallied and somehow stood up just in time to dodge a blow dealt by the Leech that was lying in wait for her. The armoured tail swung around once more and this time hit her back really hard. It was like being slammed into a concrete wall! Her back hurt and it felt as if the skin had gotten torn in a hundred places. The leech's tail had hook like projections which had cause her much harm. Not daunted by the encounter, however, Tanya swung her machine pistol at the leech's head and delivered a five second burst even as she ran out of ammunition. The last monster in the first day wilted as the bullets struck home, but not before it had managed to Tanya in the back with its tail. She somehow nursed herself to the finishing line wondering if she would still have the strength to fight the next day's fight!

Day Two

Waking on the second day of the game, Tanya could still feel the pain of the previous day's assault. She, however noticed that the wound, virtual though it might have been was fully healed. The task before her on the second day was of clearing the skies of flying Pterodactyls that were intent on grabbing her in order to take her to their nests, so to feed them to their chicks. This time she had no problems in fending off the attacks of the Pterodactyls that floated on the thermals as she was herself dressed in a flying suit with an electric motor attached to help her fly further. She had managed to fend off their attacks, firing with her machine pistol watching their wings crumple in mid-air, tumbling down into a deep void that was surrounded by jagged rocks guaranteed to smash open skulls and smash bones to pulp! But then the more Pterodactyls she killed, the more appeared in the air. She managed to end the task, tired and exhausted by the ordeals that she had faced. Just when she thought she had killed the last one, she saw a giant bird come swinging towards her. Tanya had by now exhausted most of her ammunition and it seemed that the battery pack that powered her flying suit had almost drained out.

Tanya knew that unless she did something immediately, things would turn out badly for her. Turning her attention to the scene below, she noticed that she was flying over a massive plateau, a flat surface in the mountains. Making a swift dive, she landed on the flat surface of the plateau. The giant Pterodactyl had sharp eyes however, and it also followed Tanya down. The Pterodactyl, however had no intention of landing on the flat surface, and instead it angled itself for a raking dive. Tanya realised what the huge bird had intended to and so she fell down on her back with her automatic machine gun in her hands. By now she knew that she had a few bullets left so she delayed firing at the swiftly descending Pterodactyl till the last moment. Just when the flying monster was just above her, Tanya let go with all she had. A deafening barrage almost stunned her, the blue smoke stung her eyes, and then she felt the sharpened claws of the Pterodactyl hook into her flying suit, and then she felt herself being lifted up in the air.

When she came to, Tanya was assailed by a terrible stink of rotting carrion flesh, and then she stirred, turning her head sideways, opened her eyes only to see that she was surrounded by Pterodactyl chicks! Even as she looked on, one of the chicks came hopping and stopped before her face. It poked its snout into Tanya's face, but then she decided to lie still and not move at all. She knew that if she did not do anything immediately, she would be chick feed. There was no way she could fight back the mother Pterodactyl so the only line of action would be to resort to the abort option. The players of Driven could use the abort option only thrice throughout the game and since Tanya had not used this option before; she decided to go ahead and opt for it. Feeling in the pockets of her flying suit, she came across the cylindrical canister that was known as the abort grenade. She fished out the grenade and then pulled out the safety pin, counted till three and then flung the object away. The grenade landed in the distance, and before it flashed was gobbled by one of the chicks. Tanya watched the pterodactyl chick swallow the grenade and then there was a loud explosion and the chick burst into pieces. Even before she slipped into unconsciousness, Tanya saw the mother Pterodactyl swooping towards them squawking in alarm and anger.

Tanya woke up in the relative safety of the game chamber. She had aborted the game just in time because it had seemed to her that there was no point in continuing any more. The viewers of Driven agreed that Tanya had done the right thing and they waited for the next episode to begin.

Day Three

Tanya Bhojwani woke up to the loud and gut wrenching roars of a wild animal. The task before her that day was that of finding and killing a particularly aggressive sabre-toothed tiger. For that task she was equipped with an exoskeleton suit of carbon fibre, although whether it would save her from the fangs of the sabre toothed tiger was highly questionable, and she was given a long sword as a weapon of offence. She had hardly woken up when she was driven .deep into the woods away from the advancing monster. Not having had anything to eat, Tanya was weakened and desperate to conserve her energies. Finally, after having stumbled through the thick overgrowth, she tripped and fell on to the ground before the advancing sabre toothed tiger. Weakened by hunger and thirst, Tanya waited for the killing stroke. All this while she thought about her father admitted in hospital, struggling with cancer. She thought of her mother, a woman who had given her all to keep the family together and then she thought of her boyfriend, whom she had hoped to marry one day. Tiger had reached her, its' foul breath over powered her and she just lay cowering in the undergrowth. Just when the tiger was a few paces from her, Tanya managed to lift her long sword aiming it at the belly of the tiger. What happened next was that the wild beast lunged at her, and in that moment, the lion face appeared to her with eyes glaring. She thought her time had come, and then the monster was on her. She felt a searing pain as the fangs of the tiger pierced exoskeleton her armour. The pain was excruciating. Tanya came to after a few moments only to see the sabre toothed tiger rolled to one side, her long sword sticking into its chest. In a moment of lucidity, she saw how it must have happened-the tiger had lunged at her and in the process impaled itself on to the tip of the long sword. The body armour that she wore had prevented the tiger's claws from piercing her body, but then she was left badly bruised all over her body, especially her upper chest.

By the third day the viewership ratings of the Stingray Channel that aired Tanya's virtual battles had shot up! People had begun to sit up to watch a feisty Indian girl battle her way through obstacles and tasks, scraping through each one, bruised but victorious. People had begun to bet on her chances of reaching the final round, some had even bet on whether she would come out of the game sane and healthy in mind. All this while, Kartik followed each episode with eagerness, watching each move she made, he watched her face closely to see how Tanya fared, looking for signs of weakness or signs of strength. He wanted to know whether she suffered. Tanya's mother too was torn between her worries for her husband and fear for the well-being of her daughter. One of the preconditions that the contestants were made to agree on was that there would be no communication between the contestant and the rest of the world.

Day Four

The task before Tanya Bhojwani on the fourth day was to dive into a sea filled with a few sharks, stingrays, octopus, and other dreadful sea monsters, including a giant squid, and a few barracuda eels and retrieve a golden medallion from one of the pirate ships lying on the bottom. For the day she was equipped with a compact oxygen tank, and a L.A.R. re-breather which would provide her with an almost inexhaustible supply of air. The task given to her on this day seemed to be to her liking and she took to the water like the fish that she was, but soon realised that things were not quite right. Once she felt something slimy slippery rub against her calves. Tanya had her hands full with the underwater javelin held in one hand, a hunting knife in the other, strapped and attached by a strong rubber band (a spare hunting knife she wore on her waist in a sheath. As she kept swimming towards the wreck, she swam too close to the rocks where the barracuda eel lived and what happened next was that she saw a blur as something huge lunged at her. She panicked and in that instant felt something snap at her receding legs as she frantically kicked her legs. There was suddenly a sharp pain in the back of her right leg, the calf as she felt teeth bite in. Luckily for her, the barracuda eel had managed to sink a few of its fangs into her calve and had torn the skin open. She panicked as she saw the trail of blood that she left behind her knowing that it would attract some of the underwater predators. Tanya had put on a protective swimming wet suit that could self-heal itself and soon indeed she observed as the rent in the suit repaired itself although she wondered about her wound and whether it would continue to bleed. While she was still a few hundred metres from the ship-wreck, she came across the giant octopus staring at her with baleful eyes as it rested on the bottom of the sea, quietly waiting for something to swim by. This time she was waiting only for one or two of the Octopus tentacles to come swimming at her, but then what happened finally was that a bunch of four long and ugly tentacles came searching for her. She looked at the suckers and then shuddered with disgust and horror. Each tentacle had a life of its own, and seemed to act independently of the body. When the first tentacle came glancing past, she hacked at it with her knife, struggling to regain her stance. The tentacle went spiralling down, wriggling and writhing. She had hardly hacked at one tentacle when the next came groping for her and then another and another! She knew very well that if she came into contact with any of the tentacles, it would mean certain death. Soon she was fighting for life in the midst of a sea of tentacles and while she was fending off a combined attack by the tentacles on her right, a tentacle had managed to stick itself to her left wrist. The sucker had stuck to her suit and she felt herself being dragged away by the octopus. Tanya thought about her options, cut her suit off, hack at her hand to free herself, or, 'wait, why not hack at the tentacle with my knife?' she thought as she brought her knife around carefully lest she should provide the flat side to one of the suckers, and hacked at the tentacle intending to cut it in one stroke. Immediately she felt the tugging on her wrist slacken as the rest of the tentacle fell off, but then the piece of tentacle that she had hacked was still attached to her wrist writhing and twisting with a demonic sense of urgency. Tanya now turned her attention towards the open space that had formed ahead of her after she had hacked the second tentacle and in a flash swam towards that open space and sailed through.

On reaching the shipwreck she found an entry point through the gaps in the planks of the deck and swam through one of those straight into the strong room in the next to the Captain's cabin. Inside the strong room she saw the doors of the safe were open feeling confident, she swam towards the safe not seeing the Sting-Ray lying on the floor of the cabin. The Sting ray was perfectly camouflaged because the colour of its skin merged with that of the sand-strewn deck of the ship. She had never expected to see a sting-ray lurking on the flooring of the cabin of the shipwreck! Tanya was only a few feet away when she saw the unmistakable Delta shape in the muck on the floor of the strong room and froze where she was, a difficult task since she could not arrest her momentum in a frictionless environment. Nevertheless, Tanya launched herself over the stingray hoping that she had not disturbed it in its sleep! Landing on the other side of the sting ray, next to the swinging doors of the safe, Tanya peeped into the depths of the safe and saw to her relief that the golden medallion was indeed there. She grabbed at it and then put it into the pouch she carried tied around her waist and proceeded to swim out of the strong room, through the gaps in the planking of the deck above her.

She had managed to swim above the sting ray without making too much of a disturbance in the water, the sting ray continued to sleep, or perhaps it was pretending to be asleep, waiting for the unwary victim to step on its sting!

The task set before Tanya on the fourth day had been a tough one, more so because the designers of the game had known that she was in her elements when she was in water. Tanya was aware of this and so she became doubly alert as she swam towards land, away from the wreck, not trusting the tranquillity of scene before her, the crystal clear water, colourful coral on the sea bed, a shoal of colourful tropical fish swimming by, their colours so hypnotic that she couldn't pull her eyes away! And it was while she was lost in the beauty of the sea that she was suddenly jolted back into alertness. Far away, beyond the shipwreck in the distance, she could see a massive shape emerging. It was moving towards her, growing larger and larger. A giant shark, such that none could imagine was going to be her final test. Tanya knew that she could in no way defend herself against the cold blooded beast and made a dash for the beach. She realised that if she had spent more time admiring the corals and the shoals of fish, then she would never have been able to outrun the shark. Swim is what she did, a mad rush for safety even as she sobbed for her mother. The corals and the shoals of fish had been deliberately released in order to slow her down and to make her lower her guard for a few crucial moments within which the shark would emerge and attack her. A few hundred metres from the safety of the beach, a warning siren sounded in her ears warning her that she was out of air. The re-breather had failed and to her dismay she noted that there was none left in the bottles of Oxygen strapped to her back.

Tanya was known for her ability to take prompt decisions when faced by unpredictable events. She was dubbed, 'Miss Resourceful' by her friends on many occasions, and her teachers too liked her for being, 'cool' even in the most difficult of situations! It was therefore, in keeping with her character that Tanya unclipped the L.A.R. Re-Breather and struck for the surface. Immediately she shot through the water, released by the dead weight of the cylinders and the Re-Breather. The reduced drag meant that she was able to shoot ahead of the advancing shark tumbling on to the sands of the beach gasping and spluttering and she turned back towards the sea in time to see the shark's snout breaking out of the water, chopping at the air in frustration.

The world was fascinated by Tanya's achievements on the fourth day, and the views of important and famous people were aired on television channels. Already speculation was rife that Tanya would be able to manage all the tasks very well. The cynics and detractors however warned that there were still three more tasks before Tanya, and it would be better if they reserved their opinions till the end. To add more emotion to the live telecast, the promoters of the game decided to record interviews of Tanya's mother, her classmates, and teachers. These interviews were then telecast on various channels throughout the world. The TRP ratings of the channel providing live feed of the Driven Game shot up so much that people had stopped viewing other channels and sat glued to their screens looking at Tanya fighting through all odds. Even the news channels began to air live clippings of her fighting through the tough odds. Tanya had become a teenage icon and her pictures began to appear on tee-shirts and other sports equipment with the tagline, 'Fight till Death!'

Day Five

By the fifth day into the game, Tanya was exhausted and nearing the end of her patience. She was sickened by her surroundings, the smell of ionised air, frying electric circuits and processors working overtime as the engineers tried to overclock them. Few contestants had crossed the third stage, and till then, the computers had managed very well, what with the limited simulations that were required by the third stage. The developers of the game had few options left before them. Tanya, like the computers before her was really tired by now, so when she was woken up by the virtual voice, it was with great reluctance that she took in the details of the task before her. The task set before her for the fifth day was that of rescuing a couple of travellers from a particular region in a national reserve forest where their plane had crashed. Incidentally it was a quarantined area because of a deadly strain of virus that had been brought in by an alien spacecraft. The virus, when it entered the body of the victim would take over the victim's brain and cause him or her to attack as many uninfected people as possible. The infected victims grew knife like claws on the backs of their hands. These could be projected or retracted at will. Sharp as razors, these claws could be used to inflict wounds on others, and at the same time infect the wounds with a strain of the deadly virus that was carried by the already infected carrier.

The only weapons Tanya was given were her favourite hunting knife and a PPK Walther Pistol. Besides these, she carried a radio for contacting the handlers to whom she would be handing over the two passengers. Tanya would also be using the radio to contact the two passengers. She had nothing in the way of vaccines or a bio=hazard suit to save her from potential infection. The only thing she could do to prevent possible infection was to avoid any kind of physical contact with the two passengers. Finally the buzzer sounded and there she was, inside a thick jungle with trees all around and very little light filtering down to the ground. Not daunted by the prospect of travelling in the dark and thick jungle, she took a sighting on the compass she had been given and started heading due north towards the wreckage of the plane that had crashed. The coordinates of the crash site had been fed into the radio locater, and she made good progress reaching the crash site all twelve noon having started at ten in the morning.

She discovered the two passengers squatting close to the fuselage of the plane, and she hailed them, and they answered back with yells of excitement. When she drew closer, she was shocked to see that one of them was none other than her boyfriend, Kartik, while the other was Rohan, another of her admirers whom she would have taken up as a boyfriend if Kartik had not come to her before. The two of them who had till know seemed to be at ease with each other had become suddenly very hostile and the air of animosity between them became perceptible. Kartik got up from his crouching position and advanced towards Tanya with the intention of hugging her, but then Tanya stepped back and Rohan seemed to smile when he saw that Tanya had rejected her lover. Tanya was surprised why the makers of the game had deliberately brought in her boyfriend. She believed that the contrast had specifically mentioned that there would be no contact between the players of the game and their relatives or friends, and here were Kartik and Rohan.

'But why, Tanya?' shouted Kartik in a tone of disbelief.

'Sorry, Kartik, you might have become infected by that alien virus brought by the space craft!' replied Tanya.

'Of course, Kartik,' Rohan sniggered; she has rejected you for someone else, what would she do with an engineer like you? Tanya has become a popular personality and she could have a pick of much better placed young men like you!'

Kartik dashed towards where Rohan was squatting and hurling himself at Rohan, began to punch and kick at him, all the time screaming, 'To hell with you, Rohan! You know she is my girlfriend and she can think of no one else besides me!' He stopped punching Rohan and then turned towards Tanya for support and then continued hitting Rohan.

In a moment of understanding, Tanya could see what the makers of the Driven game were attempting. They had set her up in a clever game of conflict of loyalties, and were playing with her mind! She felt really angry when she saw what the makers of the game had done. First and foremost they had dared to enter into her private life, and they would attempt to examine how loyal she was to Kartik. They would tempt her to hug and kiss Kartik in the process infecting herself with the deadly virus which would steadily sap away her strength leaving her too weak to stand up to the challenges put before her. She also could see how introducing Kartik into the game would present before her a situation that would destroy her emotionally. She was aware however, that Kartik and Rohan were present as virtual characters and not the real ones.

A sharp cry of pain brought her to the present and she turned towards the struggling duo. Tanya lifted her pistol and fired one shot into the air. The loud crack of the pistol brought the struggle between the two men to a stop and Kartik looked at Tanya with disbelief, 'You fired that gun at us, Tanya, how could you do that?'

'Look, Kartik and Rohan, I need to hand you over to your handlers. We don't have time to waste, just get up and follow me, she said waving her pistol in the direction that she had come for.

'Ha ha,' laughed Rohan, 'she doesn't want you any more Kartik,' retorted Rohan.

'Just shut up Rohan!' Shouted Tanya 'Let's move,' she shouted.

In the meantime, both Kartik and Rohan lodged their strong protest against the Game makers of Driven when they saw their lookalikes taking part in the game. They knew they were chimeras, virtual creations but still they violated their personal rights. Their protests were overruled by competent authorities who that stated that the characters of Rohan and Kartik had been extracted from Tanya's own mind they were virtual creations and not the real people, and moreover, the makers of the game argued that Tanya had signed the contract in which clause number forty-five clearly stated that the contestant was willingly surrendering his or her memory bank to provide characters and events to further the game. Their protests fell flat on deaf ears and Kartik looked with horror as the game took a rather personal tone Tanya being thrust into a situation where she had to choose between her boyfriend, the targets of the game, and the option of ditching him for Rohan.

'How much further do we have to walk?' Rohan panted.

'Just get on, you are slowing us down!' Kartik retorted.

'Not much of a distance left,' quipped Tanya.

It was almost when they had reached the point of the handover as indicated by the GPS, that she saw both the men start fighting again. She had elected to be the last in the line and had instructed Kartik to lead. Even as she started to move towards the two fighting men, she was horrified to see that Kartik had extended his razor claws and had begun to hack into Rohan. Rohan had succumbed to his injuries well before Tanya had reached them. In a moment of lucidity Tanya knew what she had to do, and cocking her pistol she aimed it at her boyfriend. Kartik looked at her with disbelief and muttered, 'You can't do that, Tanya, I dare you to!' Without a thought she shot him twice, once in the head and a second time in the chest.

The whole world gasped as they looked at their T.V. sets at the scene where Tanya had shot dead her boyfriend! The TRP ratings shot off scale, but Kartik felt sad at the outcome of the fifth task. However he contented himself with the thought that after all, Tanya didn't have any other alternative!

Day Six

The sixth day found Tanya repulsed and disgusted by the game. In fact she wanted to quit from the game, but then common sense dictated that she should complete what she had started. The task before her seemed simple enough-she was to rescue a young man from the clutches of members of a famous tribe what was known to kidnap hapless victims who stepped into their forests as proof of their prowess, these men had kidnapped one of the members of a science expedition that had been cataloguing animal and plant species found in a remote jungle in an African country known as Chencha. Tanya was given a makeup kit to camouflage herself, her favourite Hunter's knife and the Walther PPK pistol with a silencer. The young man whom she had to rescue was named Kebede and the place where he had been taken to was, Gidole, a settlement members of the Gujji tribe lived.

Tanya had also been informed that the Tribal chief, Gurage had decided to take up another wife, and in order to do this he had divorced his first wife and had become romantically attached to the eighteen year old daughter of the witch doctor in the next village with whom he had fallen in love while visiting the witch doctor whose name was Shiba Komata for the treatment of a particularly embarrassing outbreak of itchy rashes on his private parts. Shiba had treated Gurage for a good couple of months and when the treatment was over, he was reluctant to leave the witch doctor and his daughter. When Gurage asked the witch doctor for his daughter's hand in marriage, the witch doctor rebuffed him for being too old to handle his daughter who went by the name Yeromnesh. Thus angered by this insult to his manhood, Gurage the chief had decided to undergo the trial required of young grooms who were eager to get married. They had to prove themselves by furnishing proof of their manhood in the form of trophies cut from the bodies of their victims. Kebede was to be the trophy that was to be presented before the witch doctor's daughter as proof of his manhood!

Deep in her mind, Tanya suspected that the makers of the virtual game Driven were up to something rather fishy, otherwise why they would have sent her into the depths of a jungle. Being a tall and athletically built woman, she was being sent into the depths of Africa to rescue and African man from the clutches of a romantically besotted tribal chief! Anyway, she couldn't do anything about this, could she? When the second last task was announced, the viewers speculated about the outcome of the game. Many claimed that Tanya would end up becoming the wife of the chief; others felt that she would be slaughtered by the men of the Gujji Tribe. A few reserved their opinions for later on, while Kartik suffered a feeling of intense disgust about the manner in which the makers of the virtual game Driven were manipulating things.

Tanya was dropped a couple of kilometres away from Gidole at ten in the morning. She started advancing towards the settlement using the trees, as hiding places. She had just reached the boundary of the settlement made of a ring of thorny scrubs when she heard the sound of a band of men approaching her. She had left the forest cover way behind her and looked helplessly for cover; there was none. Soon the men came into site and on seeing her, they literally pounced on her leaving her no time to draw her weapons. She saw that it was no use struggling against these men who were lean, muscular and more than six feet tall. After she stopped fighting them, the men started groping her, hands slipping into her blouse and hands pawing at her breasts. All this time the men were calling out excitedly to each other announcing that they had caught hold of a female intruder. One of the men discovered the cosmetic case and on opening it notice the bottles lined in it. Being curious he opened the cap. On seeing nothing coming out of it, he lifted it into the air peering through the tiny hole only to be shocked when a cloud of black powder poured onto his face making the others pause what they were doing. Looking at the man's face, everyone started laughing. It was at this moment that a voice of authority barked at them, and they immediately stood up as a singularly ugly looking fellow began to advance towards them. He was fat, his belly distended, his eyes yellowed with jaundice, teeth blackened with decay and as he walked towards the young men, he belched and farted loudly! The young men knew better than to laugh, but then Tanya could scarcely hold her laughter.

'Hah, hah, what do I zee heere?' he panted as he saw Tanya lying on the ground. Seeing her at close quarters, Gurage, (that is who he was) saw that he had been rewarded with a comely woman who had a fair skin and looked exotic. 'You be my wife!' he grunted and with that instructed the young men to take her to his hut. Once there, Tanya was relieved of her pistol and her hunting knife and thrown onto the ground. She lay on the ground for a few moments, cursing herself for having allowed herself to be caught, and now she was going to be forcefully married to that man! A good half hour later, the door opened, and a young girl about her own age stepped in with a bowl of what looked like lumps of dumplings swimming in a thick soup.

'You eat this…Kurkuffa…you strong, you marry soon!' the girl said pointing towards herself, 'me Zenabish-chief's daughter!'

Tanya knew better than to argue with her, and instead she smiled at her and said, 'I am Tanya, and I am from a faraway land!'

'You will be my step mother,' said Zenabish.

'But I am only as old as you are, I can't marry your father just now!' exclaimed Tanya as she ate into the dumplings.

After she had had her meal, Gurage and his advisor paid her a visit making it known that he would be marrying her that night. Tanya however made it known that she would marry him on the condition that he brings her a man from the nearest town intact. Gurage looked at her with suspicion for he didn't want his new wife spoiled by any one. It was strange that in a land of strange customs and traditions much importance was given to the virginity of women before marriage. Tanya's stubbornness however convinced the chief to bring in the young man whom they had kidnapped.

When they had brought the young man into her presence, they expressed their reluctance in allowing Tanya and Kebede alone. But then Tanya made it known that the guards could stay in the room and she took Kebede to one side to talk to him. Kebede was himself shocked to see her in that desolate place in Africa, and after a moment's hesitation said, 'Tum yaha kyan kar rahe ho?' (What are you doing here? in perfect Hindi). He told her that he had studied Zoology in one of the colleges in Delhi. Speaking in Hindi meant that the guards didn't know what they were talking about. Finally after telling him that she was a contestant in the virtual game 'Driven' and this was her sixth task she set before him their plan of action. She would tell the chief to release Kebede a good four hours before the marriage which was to take place at eight. Kebede then would make for the town from where he had been kidnapped. Tanya would in the meantime ask for her cosmetic case to be brought and on getting it, she would select one of the bottles which contained concentrated nitric acid which she would pour on to the hinges that linked the wooden door to the jamb.

Finally Gurage agreed to this, reluctantly at first but then agree he finally did when he saw that Tanya was absolutely stubborn. Everything went on as planned; Kebede was released at four in the evening. Tanya took her time in dressing up, not really wearing the white cotton gown given to her. Little after seven the chief's daughter came into the hut where Tanya had been imprisoned and looked at where the white cotton gown was folded on the mat. She sniffed at the pungent smell of the acid reacting with the iron hinges but then readily went away the bucket of water Tanya had demanded making it clear to her that she needed to wash her face.

The sixth task ended in a farce when the Chief no longer able to wait to get to his soon to be wed wife discovered that the bird had flown the coop and when he realised that she was nowhere to be found, he decided to replace her with his earlier love, the daughter of the witch doctor. But then in order to wed the witch doctor's daughter he had to present to the witch doctor the young man as a trophy. The men suddenly realised that they had themselves released the young man, Kebede a good four hours earlier. Gurage sent some of his best men in pursuit of Kebede and if possible the dream girl he had set his eyes on. The men set out into the night, but returned empty handed the next morning. Both Tanya and Kebede had escaped unscathed!

Day Seven, the day of Reckoning

The final day had come, and Tanya was now going to take the final test. The test was called the ring of fire, and the contestants, none who had reached this stage were supposed to escape a circle of advancing monsters who were equipped with maces, swords, lances, spears, and daggers. Beyond the ring of advancing monsters was a ring of fire that seemed to be impenetrable. Tanya was by now resigned to the outcomes of the game. To win or lose hardly mattered to her, and she knew that she was the only contestant who had reached this far. The world as a whole was glued to the TV sets. For many it was a foregone conclusion that this spunky girl would manage this task too. Tanya's mother had spent her time in prayers and she had visited the Birla temple on Mandir Marg in Delhi to offer prayers. Tanya's boyfriend, Kartik sat in his room glued to his TV set, hoping that the girl he loved would clear this task too. The news channels aired the opinions of famous personalities who had come up with the idea that such reality shows should be brought to an end. The makers of the Virtual Game, 'Driven' felt that they had finally come to an end of a successful season of the reality show. They had incidentally thrown everything that they had at Tanya, but had to concede defeat at the hands of this resourceful teenager. They had however made a lot of money in terms of sponsorships and TRP ratings.

On the penultimate day of her virtual game, Tanya woke to a voice announcing her penultimate task. Voice had taken a kinder tone and it advised her to, 'Be alert and aware of her surroundings.' Tanya was given her Knife and a light weight sword. She would be wearing a skin hugging suit that would protect her from the heat of the fire but nothing else! Just before she entered into the portal however she saw the glaring eye of the lion, and was daunted by the glare of violence that the gaze carried within it.

Tanya found herself on an open plain surrounded by an advancing ring of monsters, and at the head of the circle she saw the majestic lion face advancing towards her. Trembling with fear, she realised that she would have to take a leap into the midst of the advancing monsters before the circle became too dense. She remembered the instructions of her gym instructor about taking leaps and running towards the advancing monsters she managed to find a gap between a gargoyle and a wolf slipping through. In the process however she felt the gargoyle's sword nick into the back of her right shoulder blade. The wolf bared its fangs and nipped into her thigh, but then she leaped through running full tilt into the advancing ring of fire. The heat of the fire was so intense that she almost fainted, her hair was singed and she felt her whole body bake in the intense heat, but then she didn't feel the pain as she exulted in the thrill of having crossed over safety. Klaxons sounded in the room declaring that she had finally managed to clear the last obstacle. Channels all over the world telecast her victory.

The world welcomed their new hero and she was given a hero's welcome by none other than the prime minister of the country. Tanya was welcomed by her mother and her boyfriend who welcomed her back into the real world. The organisers of the virtual game, 'Driven' became bankrupt after paying Tanya her prize money, but then they were happy in a way for having won recognition in the world of virtual games.

Tanya woke up after a few days to a world that recognised her for her resourcefulness and presence of mind. The prize money that she won went into the treatment of her father, and there was enough money left from the treatment to provide for all her needs till the day she died. Tanya enrolled in one of the colleges and did her B.B.A followed by an M.B.A. She became a successful manager in one of the multinational companies and got married to her boyfriend, Kartik. It went without saying that Tanya had become a bigger teenage icon than the most revered of cricket players. Tanya and Kartik went on to have two children, son and a daughter. Tanya's father recovered from his ailment and went on to lead a healthy life till he died of natural causes at the age of seventy five. Her courage and bravery would soon become an inspiration for all young people across the globe. Finally bowing down to public outrage, the Government finally banned virtual reality games such as 'Driven'.

Note: This short story appeared as a supplement in my Novel, The Other Side of Love, Beyond a Shadow of Doubt as an unedited and incomplete story titled, 'Driven'.

Anecdotes

Spitting Cobras and
Toads Come in Pairs!

The children were sitting around me, begging for a story before they turned into their camp beds in the adventure camp they were all grade ten boys and girls. I had already told them about the real incident when a spitting cobra had entered our sitting room in a town called Arbaminch and my father had had to kill it because he was worried for our safety, my brother's, my mother's and mine. I was already exhausted by the day's activities which had included an arduous trek in the mountains close to Dehradun a few kilometres from Mussoorie, followed by rappelling down a cliff face and slithering down one of the iron bridges on to a river. The children insisted that I should stick to my promise – there was no escape for me, I was stuck! As it is, one of the adventure guides, a lithe girl named Reshma looked towards me with eager eyes.

'Why don't you humour them, Sir?' She interjected.

'OK, just one story, that's it!' I exclaimed, knowing that I was trapped!

'Sir, we will have just one story from you before we go off to sleep!' Said Ananya, a girl who was into dancing and fashion shows in school.

The night was still and there was the glow from the fire we had lit. Dinner had been followed by some games and now it was story time!, I had thought they would forget the promise I had made to them the previous evening but then that was not to be. Moreover, the other teacher in the group, Amina, nodded at me in encouragement.

'Fine,' I said, 'this is something that happened after that spitting cobra incident, I am sure that you will all agree that Cobras live in pairs all their lives!'

'Of course, Sir, Indian mythology describes how the Nags live in pairs, Sir!' Rakesh, the self-proclaimed medic on the trip said. Although a student of grade ten, he would suggest a dose of Aspirin for those who suffered from headache and Crocin for those with mild fever.

'Well, this incident happened a few weeks after the spitting cobra incident. My father had fully recovered from the venom that had been sprayed into his eyes, and he had to go to Addis Ababa for some important work, and to give some stuff to my uncle who was going to India. The package was meant form my grandmother who lived in Gurgaon. It was evening and my mother had to make chapattis for dinner, so she went to the kitchen which was in one of the out houses. She'd made almost all the chapattis when she heard a rustling sound coming from beneath the table on which the gas stove had been placed. Well she was a brave and alert woman and so, she very calmly stepped away from the table and looked beneath the table to where a couple of used car tyres had been kept. On looking closely, she noticed the head of a cobra peeping out from one of the tyres, of course she knew it was a cobra after it all it was only a week after the incident in which a spitting cobra had spat on my father. The snake stuck itself out of the tyre well and reared itself up to a height of about a foot and a half. My mother hastily withdrew calmly out of the kitchen and then fled to the main building. Once away from the kitchen, she called out to one of the boys, a student who lived in another outhouse. Keffne as he was named called out to some more young boys nearby, and armed with sticks and a torch, they rushed to the kitchen. When they reached there however, they found no sign of the snake. The tyre well was empty, and it became clear that the snake had fled the scene!'

'So what do you think had happened?' Shamita, another of the students who was sitting in the group asked me. 'Don't you think your mother might have imagined the whole thing?' She asked with a rather cynical tone.

'No, my mother had indeed seen a snake, a cobra for that effect, and to add to it all was the fact that lone snake was seen during the following days doing the round of the house. The snake did not harm anyone, and after a week, it went away.'

'So what?' Sarthak quipped. He was a strapping boy, who was also the school's renowned athlete.

'Well,' I continued, 'after my father returned from Addis Abeba, a couple of days after the incident, my mother described everything to him. After listening to the whole incident quietly, he told us that it was the mate that had come looking for its pair. According to him, it was probably the female companion of the snake he had killed a few weeks earlier.'

It was getting rather late, and I just wanted to go off to sleep, but then it was clear that the children thought I was trying to fob them off with a lame story! To make matters worse for me, Reshma, the adventure guide turned to me and said, 'Surely, you cannot claim that it was the companion of the snake your father had killed a few weeks earlier, Sir!'

I replied to her, 'We believed, all of us, that the snake had come looking for its partner, and when it couldn't find its partner it just went away!' I replied hoping that was the end of the whole matter. I beat a hasty retreat to my hut hoping to turn in for the night in peace, but that was not to be! After what seemed to be a half hour of peace in the camp, loud screams rent the air from the batch of huts that housed the boys. I rushed to the hut from which the boys - four in number were sleeping, and when I entered, I asked them what the matter was. One of the boys gestured towards the floor and following his pointing hand I glanced at the sight that must have appeared most funny to the students. Barely containing myself, I darted into the bathroom to grab a broom, for there in full sight was a pair of toads close to each other, they were the most ugly toads I had ever seen in my life. The toads looked back at the students with what was an utmost lack of a sense of concern or even fear! Ironically, the boys were more afraid of the toads than the toads were of them! Quietly, with a poker faced expression, I swept away the pair of toads into the bathroom and from there freedom! 'Sure,' I thought to myself, 'they certainly live in pairs, the toads and snakes!'

That night, I was not able to get any rest, for the moment I returned to my hut and had barely laid down to sleep when there was a lot of whispering and commotion at my door. When I opened my door to enquire about the nature of the commotion, I got to know from a couple of boys that one of their companions had vomited. On visiting the boy's tent, it became clear that the hapless fellow had ingested copious amounts of chips and fried snacks and on top of that he had drunk a bottle of an aerated drink. To make matters worse he had not had any dinner! Fortunately, our self-proclaimed medic, Rakesh had given him fruit salts and that was the end of the whole matter. I returned to my hut thinking it was all over, and thankfully laid down to sleep when another scream rent the night. I bolted out of my hut and rushed to the boys' hut from which the scream had emanated. On getting the door opened, I was able to see what was wrong, the boys had screamed on seeing a massive spider crawling across the wall. Once again, maintaining an appearance of utmost cool, I grabbed hold of the broom and shooed the offending arachnid out of sight, into the bathroom. I bid them 'good night' and then shut the door before me.

I finally retired to my hut deprived of my sleep and part of my dignity, for not only had my story been questioned for authenticity and veracity, but also because of the fact that I had to remove the two toads that were the human equivalent of husband and wife from in front of the boys. Of course they must have known what the toads were doing; I wondered if they had not called me to their room just to see me embarrassed! The only sounds that came from the huts that housed the girls were sounds of derision and mockery! It was as if they had known what was happening in the boys' rooms and they were making fun of the boys who were scared of two toads and a spider that was just passing by!

A Student who wanted to learn rules of Grammar

The group of teachers insisted that I tell them stories from my life as a teacher and there was no other option but to tell them about a few incidents that had left a mark on my memory. That day was the last day of the retreat that had been organised by the institution where we had been serving. It had been a hectic day of winding up exchanging notes and packing up so I felt a little lethargic but anyway, I obliged them. We had had a late session and had dinner quite late, at about a half past ten. By then no one was ready to go off to sleep and they wanted to spend the rest of the night lying on the carpets listening to tales and anecdotes from each other. It was my turn to tell them a set of stories and there was simply no escape for me!

'It was in the year 2010 that a touching incident took place in my life as a teacher. A student came up to me with a shy smile. Well, he seemed to be smarter than the others though he was slightly built, physically!' I narrated my experience to a group of colleagues who had already described their experiences as teachers.

There was an expectant silence as if they all wanted me to continue with my story; well it was not a story, was it? 'Well, he wanted me to teach him English grammar so that he could be fluent like me. I expressed my surprise to him because very few students in those days were interested in Grammar.' My listeners stirred in their seats as if they were growing restless and wanted me to go on. 'Well, he said to me, 'I really don't know why the others don't want to learn grammar, all I know is that it interests me more than anything else!'

I continued with my narrative, 'Sure son, I will teach you the Mathematics of English so that you might be better than me.' I told him 'I felt deeply touched about his plea, because I could see how different he was from the others, especially because very few students had the hunger to learn. Most of them were only after marks and passing marks were all they wanted, but this student had a hunger for learning that I could not see in the others.

It could be seen that they were all feeling tired and were probably sitting to listen to me out of respect. 'After a few days, the same boy came to me and he asked me if I could help him write a speech on the impact of pollution on the environment, sure I helped him write the speech and it was really a good one too!' By now I had realised that I was not so good a storyteller and it was high time I backed out the promise I had made of telling them stories after dinner.

'Son, you need to practice speech writing so that you can perfect the art!' I said to the boy, and he replied, 'Sure Sir, that I will certainly do, that for I would like to be like you!' he said with a firmness that surprised me a great deal!

I guess by now I had lost the interest of the listeners it was a lost cause because in any case they were too tired to even appreciate my story, but then, I decided to carry on, 'The little boy's smile haunts me to this day, I have forgotten his name, but will probably never forget that hunger to learn! I just couldn't help wonder why the other students were not like him!'

This is how the first part of my storytelling session ended, but then none of the others ted to go to bed because they were waiting for the coffee to come! 'Tell us another story' said Vedika Sharma as if to spite me and the others by not allowing anyone to go off to sleep.

Thus it was that I then launched into yet another story about a student whom I would call from here onwards as 'The Little Boy'.

'It was in the year 2013 when I came across this particular boy who was a bit slow in catching up with what was taught in class. What irritated me as a teacher was that he stuck close to me wherever I went, it was as if he wanted to touch me, maybe this was in order to get some kind of assurance. Often, it so happened that the other boys played pranks on him and he took part in their pranks rather gamely, even if it meant that he got hurt or even became the butt of a joke!'

'And you didn't do anything to stop this, did you, Mr. Singh?' asked Ramesh Garg, the Physics teacher.

'No, it was not like this,' I replied, trying to defend myself - 'I did step in a number of times, but then it became a vicious circle; the boys would bully him just to see him make a complaint to me so that I would pull up the perpetrator of the crime,' I hesitated before continuing, 'you see, after some time it became difficult for me to keep addressing this issue at the cost of the other learners so I began to ignore the complaints after some time.'

The coffee had finally arrived and those who had begun to doze woke up the moment the scent of the coffee filled the room. 'You see we were the senior most teachers of the school who had been on a retreat at a farmhouse in Faridabad, Haryana and we had attended workshops throughout the three days we had been at the farmhouse. We would be returning home the following day after some fun activities. By the end of the third day we all sat after dinner till late in the night lying comfortably on the mattresses that had been spread on the floor of the conference room, listening to anecdotes and stories about our lives as teachers. All this took place after dinner. We were a group of three male teachers and four female teachers. I waited for everyone to have their coffee and then continued when I got a nod from a couple of my colleagues.

'One day, while we were having a Jam session as a formative tool of assessment for English and many of the louder and brash students were cowed about the jam session, the little boy came to me and said, 'I would like to go next!' I was surprised and told him to go ahead. The others started with their usual taunts and jibes which I tried very hard to suppress.' I took a sip of my coffee and so did the others, and I continued, 'What he said next literally shocked all of us, even the bullies!' I paused yet again for effect as the silence made it possible to hear the sound of the clock ticking. 'He said, 'I want to speak about how I feel in class. I want to make friends in this class but all of them avoid me! I want to be loved and cared for, but they all bully me. I really want to be a part of this class, but they won't let me!' I was shocked, and the class fell silent! And then Devina, one of the students began to clap her hands and then all of us followed suit – I gave the little boy a five on five because this was the most original and most honest extempore speech I had heard from a student of mine.'

There was an even deeper silence and I thought I might have seen a couple of the lady teachers sniffing and perhaps wiping away tears, but then it was Akash Sharma, the Hindi teacher who finally broke the silence and said, 'That was a most touching story!'

The others agreed, and Arpita, the Biology teacher added, 'Yes that was a most touching story, to think that it was the victim himself who turned the tables against the bullies – speaks volumes about the meaning of true courage!'

We all turned off to sleep, all of us lost in our thoughts.

'Yes indeed, it was a touching story!' agreed the others, except for one who was already snoring! Anyway, I did not mind it because now, I really felt tired and wanted to retire for the night, but then if only the others would suggest calling it a day! But then no one was ready to call it quits and there I was, ready to doze off, until the caffeine kicked in and then they demanded that I tell them one last anecdote before we called it quits.

And so I launched on yet another story of mine from a real life experience as a teacher in another school in Delhi. 'There was this boy whom I taught in grade eleven. He was, like the little boy a healthy boy who showed immense promise as a student. He was a student of the commerce stream. I noticed however that he had a very typical handwriting – the letters were sort of, you know rounded up. It was as if each letter was written within a circle, so the 'R' was rounded up as if it followed the inner curve of a circle. The same could be said of all the letters. It was rather strange, but then I gave it little thought at that time, though it stayed in my mind as a nagging feeling that there was something more to it. By the time the end of the session arrived, Rakesh as I will name him had begun to take a lot of leaves from school and his grades had begun to drop. His handwriting that had been legible till some time back became even more convoluted as if the imaginary circle within which each letter was written had become smaller and tighter. It was as if Rakesh had started to force his letters into smaller and smaller circles, and yes it appeared as if he was forcing the letters into the most impossible and most tight circles conceivable. Anyway, Rakesh managed to pass all his exams and he was promoted to the next grade, grade twelve. By grade twelve however Rakesh was more absent than present and yes, we were really worried about him. Each time he came to school he grew thinner and thinner. Towards the end he had become a veritable scarecrow, a mere skeleton and a shadow of what he had been once, a lively and healthy young boy. Finally it had been a whole month since we last saw him at school and then the Commerce teacher and I decided to pay him a visit at his home. We both went to his home which was near the school only to find that there was no one at home and the doors were locked. There was nothing we could do but to return to school without having gained any information about Rakesh.'

The second round of coffee round of coffee arrived and I took the much needed pause to collect my thoughts. My friends and colleagues were by now quite awake and I could see that there was no possibility of going to bed as yet!

When they had all settled in, I continued, 'Mr. Mann, the Commerce teacher later told me that he had come across Rakesh's parents and they had told him that Rakesh had died in hospital!'

'What are you saying? What happened to him?' asked Arpita.

'I am coming to that!' I said and then continued, 'When Mr. Mann asked Rakesh what had happened, they told him that their son had been suffering from a mental ailment, Schizophrenia because of which he had simply stopped eating! I was devastated by this news; it seemed to me that the handwriting had been a hint after all, something had after all been wrong with Rakesh!'

'An amazing account!' remarked Manish, the Sociology teacher who had been I thought sleeping all this time.

'Yes, I agree with you, Manish' I agreed, 'but then now I am going off to sleep, I can't stay up another minute, and moreover we have a fun filled activity tomorrow, let us recoup our energy for tomorrow, good night all of you!' I said as I got up resolutely and walked out of the conference room. There was no way that I was going to spend another minute there. I had always enjoyed spinning yarns filled with fantasy and science fiction, but then I had decided to regale them with what I thought were some of the more profound experiences from my life as a teacher. 'Serve them right!' I thought as I proceeded to my room, I had wanted to give them a few things to chew upon and if they didn't like my anecdotes, so be it!

Choorche

She was called 'Choorche', what that name meant we did not know, the kids and me! All we knew was that she was 'crazy,' it meant that you could chase her down the streets calling her out names – not that she ever seemed to bother. So lost was she in her own world, that I wondered if she even noticed us, a team of rowdy boys and girls trailing her, calling out names till she drifted out of the vicinity. In those days we lived in 'Kebele 03' – ('Kebele' meant 'locality' in Amharic) in Arbaminch, Ethiopia in times when Socialism was at its height and those who did not conform were thrown into jail or shot in the back and thrown into a mass grave. Choorche, however was beyond the strictures of the Government and she roamed the streets a free bird, exempt from community service or enforced labour. We also wondered sometimes if she might not be one of the spies employed by the government to spy on the citizens – to see whether everyone was behaving in accordance to the rules set by Karl Marx, Frederic Engels, and Vladimir Illych Lenin. Of course she was an enigma called Choorche, a feminine equivalent of the bogey man, a crazy person, or a government spy, all rolled into one! Perhaps she was a witch come to steal little boys so as to cook them in her cauldron!

It had been raining that day since morning, and the whole road in front of our house had turned into veritable sticky mulch that stuck to our shoes adding on to the weight and perhaps our height, so we decided to stay indoors. When the sun did turn up, it was to the accompaniment of vapours rising from the wet mud and a stream of fiery red velvet spiders, some round and fat, while the others were smaller and thinner. That was the day, Eskinder threw a stone at her, 'Choorche,' I mean! Eskinder and Amsalu called us out to play and mother gave us permission to go out to play provided we did not stray far, and ensured that we did not make any noise. She liked to have her afternoon siesta so, that was it.

The road in front of our house remained a sticky, treacly mess and we kept slipping and sliding on the surface. Outside our compound we were greeted by Dawit, and Simein. All of them were close friends and partners in mischief. As we proceeded towards the end of the road lead to the flea-market, we saw Choorche crossing the road towards us! Amsalu began to call out to her, trying to tease her and make her respond, but then as usual, she didn't appear to even notice him! 'You there, you, and what are you doing here?' – He shouted. Eskinder added, 'Have you come to pack one of us inside your bag?' My brother and I began to break away from the group as we sensed that something regrettable was going to take place. I gestured to my brother, Sam to break away and we both, got away from the whole group. And then it happened – we all saw the stone, the size of a duck's egg sail in the air, a lazy flight connecting in its final impact with the crazy woman's forehead. It was a glancing blow, but it did draw what seemed to be a copious amount of blood! We all stood frozen to the ground, my brother, me and all the other children. There was a hush and then the sounds of the world came back and there, we saw Choorche walk away, as unconcerned and aloof as ever! We had seen blood, but then after some time it had disappeared! Amsalu and Eskinder jogged towards the woman to see where the wound on her forehead had gone, and lo, they noticed that her forehead bore no mark whatsoever! It was as if the stone had never hit her at all!

'What now,' I said to Amsalu, 'do we tell our parents about this strange incident?'

He shrugged his shoulders, 'Well, I guess nobody will believe in our whole story, in fact they will think we have gone mad!

How do you explain the incident of a stone striking the forehead of a tramp, seeing the blood from the wound pour out and then noticing after a few moments that there was no scar at all? We lived in a state of fear for a couple of days and then decided that our lives would have to go on. In those days it was really difficult not to live in a state of fear the police would do should they come to know of the incident. Moreover we were scared of the scolding our parents would give us when they heard that one of our friends had thrown a stone at a helpless woman!

When we saw Choorche next week, we made it a point to steer away from her; however much we tried to avoid her, she kept marching towards us! This was about morning, about nine, and we were there, the whole gang, my brother – Sam, Amsalu, Eskinder, Tesfaye, and Dawit. We were somehow able to break away from her and then decided to take a walk towards the Senior Secondary School. The group had added one more member, Tadesse, our helper and a student of grade eleven joined us saying he had some work at school. We also took the one bicycle we had and took turns to ride it. That day we took the main road, the highway instead of the inner lane. As we started walking towards the school and away from the town, we had reached about halfway through when we saw yet another group of friends take the road behind us. I guess they too were headed towards the Senior Secondary School. Wondwosen and his sister, Tigiste, both son and daughter of the head clerk lived in the houses at the beginning of the lane, they were our neighbours.

That day we had somehow begun talking about life and death, Tadesse took the lead and told us about how death wasn't the end of life and stuff that somehow fascinated and repelled us at the same time. Even as we were moving towards the Senior Secondary School where my brother and I studied and my parents taught, there was a sense of gloom and sadness in the air, it was as if that something bad was going to take place. Moments after we had crossed the road and were on the side where the school was located, there was a loud bang followed by a screech of brakes. It all happened in slow motion, we saw a Land rover hit Tigist and then saw her flying in the air. The vehicle then skidded on the gravel towards the gully on the right and then it tipped over. Wondwosen had managed to cross the road before his sister, but she had somehow gotten confused the moving vehicle and had been hit.

The two men crawled out of the vehicle, fear writ large on their faces! Seeing that they were alright, we rushed, all of us to the spot where the impact had taken place. It was all over for Tigiste, her skull had been smashed in. That was the first time that we had as children, seen death at close quarters. For days, nay months we were deeply affected, no devastated by what we had witnessed! Our exuberance, noisiness and garrulousness had been tamed by what we had seen. We often wondered if Choorche had been trying to tell us something when she was rushing towards us and we just ran away.

It had been some time since we had retired into a feeling of sadness and grief, and hadn't seen Choorche for ages, so when one day we finally saw her enter the other end of our lane, we rushed to cheer and jeer at her. Life was back to normal, and Choorche had ensured that we would regain our cheerfulness. Looking at those moments, we wondered if our cruelty to her, was not perhaps expected of children, for boys will be boys and children will always be children! That day when Amsalu and Eskinder ran up to her to call out names, they were scolded by an elderly man who went on to take them to task for harassing an innocent person. Embarrassed and chagrined, the two of them beat a hasty retreat and joined us on the other side of the lane. After a few days, the children stopped harassing Choorche, and they accepted her as a fact of life.

The tragedy that had taken place on the highway had somehow changed our attitude towards Choorche. We stopped throwing sticks or stones at her any more. More often than not, some elder person stepped in to shoo us away from Choorche before the heckling became something worse. Looking in retrospect, it is clear that Choorche was neither a witch, nor a spy working for the Government, she was just a woman who was lost in her thoughts, she had retreated so deep into the depths of her mind that nothing from the outer world would ever reach her consciousness. The ritual of heckling and calling out to her had perhaps become a routine that she had accepted as one of the duties of her life, and for us boys, it was a celebration of being alive and healthy!

Special Children

I t was my turn to spend time with the Special Children that day. I had looked forward to that day because I was curious to know more about these special children some of whom were autistic. I reached the Enrichment Centre on time and the moment I walked down the corridor to my assigned class, I was greeted most enthusiastically by other special children who were in their classes. The five students of the class assigned to me were to reach at 8:45 a.m.(classes for the normal children started at 8:00 a.m.). In the meantime I was briefed about all the five students who were in their early teen, three boys and two girls. After the briefing, (which included a description about the schedule for the day) I accompanied one of the two teachers to the main-gate to welcome the children. At the gate, I was introduced to many other special children. One girl a student of the class to which I had been assigned seemed to be in a particularly cheerful mood, she had a mischievous twinkle in her eyes, and sang a number of popular Hindi film songs all the way to the classroom. Many of the children we met at the gate were special in some way or the other. There was this particular boy who walked on his toes. When I asked the teacher accompanying me, why it was that he walked on his toes, she told me that he was Autistic and he felt more secure walking on his toes. There was another boy who had been accompanied by his parents. He became agitated the moment he saw his parents walk away. I could see the tenderness in his father's eyes, who didn't want to leave his son. It was the mother, however, who was made of sterner stuff who spoke sharply to the father telling him to leave the son. When I asked the special education teacher, she told me that the fear of his parents leaving him behind was the cause of his agitation. A few days ago, the parents had left him with his grandparents for a few days and this had put a sense of insecurity in his mind.

After we had escorted the five children to the class, Sam was assigned to me. He seemed to be a rather intelligent boy although I was told that he was autistic like the other four. After introductions were over, and everyone greeted me with smiles, Veronica kept on staring at me! She had a rather sweet voice, bright intelligent eyes and a wonderful accent, although she spoke a few words at a time. After this we sang the school prayer and then went out for assembly. Each child carried a board with his or her name on it, and these boards were placed on the ground and the children stood on them. The students, after returning to their class then went on to identify the day, date, month, and year. First period for Sam was work experience so he led me to the Carpenter's Workshop. His assignment was to cut four pieces of wood and then to plane them with a planer. I had a wonderful time helping him saw those pieces of wood and planning them. At the workshop I met many other special children, some of whom I had seen in the library on various days. They were all curious about me, and so were their teachers. One particular boy came to me and rather excitedly showed me his colourful jacket. Another boy kept looking at me, intelligence gleamed in his eyes. His teacher later told me that he wanted to know more about me, and she told me that once he came to know my name, he would search for information about me from the internet. I told him to go ahead and tell me the next day what he had found out about me. And yes, I told him that I taught English!

Post the first period, the children returned to their classes, washed hands and then had their snacks. Sam had a computer class in the second period. I accompanied him to the Computer Lab. He was given the task of typing sentences written in a story book on the computer which he did quite accurately! For the third period we returned to class and Sam and Veronica had another task, which they mimed to me, 'walk-time'. Before I went out for this activity, I was briefed by the teacher that 'Walk Time' was an exercise in which the children were supposed to walk on a predestined path a fixed number of times. The teacher also warned me that that they had a habit of taking short cuts and not completing their five circuits. So after a brief instruction to the two children not to take a short cut, we set out to the playground. An innovative method for counting the number of circuits had been devised for them. Each time they completed a circuit, they would remove one Velcro attached red marker from the board which they carried. The red markers were then placed into the pocket attached to the board. Veronica was very excited during the walk pointing towards strange plants and herbs while Sam seemed to be more serious, concentrating on the task before him, rather like a more mature C.E.O. of a future company, what with his no-nonsense attitude!

After lunch, the fourth period was all about speech therapy, so I accompanied Mohit and Sunil both to the speech therapy room. Both of these special students had problems with speech, so the speech therapist made them practice different sounds, and some words. While Sunil had a problem saying the letter 'L', Mohit would answer only if you gave him a choice. Once the Speech therapy session was over, we returned to class where, I was then given the task of teaching Sam Maths. The Maths lesson included marking the time on a clock face, (which he incidentally did very well) followed by marking lines of a particular length with the help of a ruler, and last but not least, the children had to solve simple sums of division with the help of different objects. We also played a version of Snakes and Ladders called Snacks and Ladders. Along the way there were some rewards in the form of eatables marked by small pouches or pictures of chocolates, biscuits and wafers. The children enjoyed this game a lot. They would clap with glee when their counters landed on a space which was marked with a reward! A fine way of teaching counting and numbers, I'd say! The last period was for Occupational therapy, and Sam took me to the Occupational Therapy room where another teacher took him through different exercise routines, swinging from a ladder attached to the ceiling, pedalling, slotting wooden pieces into a cut out puzzle. It was amazing how efficiently an autistic child like Sam was able to complete each routine with such ease and confidence!

The time to bid farewell to these special children and their amazing teachers had finally come and it was with great reluctance that I left them. In days to come, and whenever I came across these children, I was amazed to observe how well they remembered me! Veronica would great me whenever she saw me, and Sam and the others would do the same too! There was a lot that I had learned from these children, and I strongly believe that all of us have some disability or the other!

An Anthology of Poems

The Boy

He was slow, and clumsy, but he had a smile all the time.
He'd come to the front and touch me by
the hand to gain attention, but I
Brushed him away, irritated at the proximity. He'd
hover around all the time asking, perhaps,
To be loved and cared for, but no one gave him a chance!

They tied his shoe laces so he fell, punched
him on his back, and thought
They had a victory, those cowards! I could see
the smug smiles on their faces, of
Satisfaction for having hit him anticipation for
more victories to come, and I was irritated.
Having little time to intervene, I went on
with the lesson as he suffered.

One day, it was his turn to deliver a speech
for just a minute, and then
Things changed forever! His topic was, 'Friends'
and he started with, 'I have no
No friends' and the whole class fell silent. And
he went on, 'I'd love to have friends

But no one would like to be friends with
me!' And the class did fall silent!

By the time his speech was ended and the whole class was sure in
Tears, but the chief bully had an even more
smug face, revelling in the tricks
Kicks and fists that he'd lash on the boy. But
angered and moved to shame did I lash
Out at him, 'Take on someone your league
not someone below you!'

That smug and overconfident look turned
to one of distaste and disgust,
'For,' I continued, 'If you pick up on someone
below you, then it means you are a
Coward, someone without guts!' And his resolve
did turn to ashes, his plans to bully
The boy abandoned, and the class looked
at him for what he was, a coward!

They now looked at the boy with new
respect, since he had voiced feelings
So honest, and moreover, none did expect him
to last a minute in a field where the
Toughest speakers had failed to make it to the
one minute time limit. And I, the learner
More than a teacher, applauded the boy and
remarked, 'Wonderful boy, well done!'

Spoils of War

As the sun sinks down into the horizon,
a silence descends on the field,
Broken only by the groans and cries of
pain of the injured, and the last
Gasps of those preparing to go away. The
sky flashes in hues of bright
Orange, pink, copper, red, and crimson -
one last time before the end!

A tide of colours does flash across the
heavens, to imitate the event that
Took place on the ground, a sad moment
when even the tough ones did
Crumple like sand castles swept away by
the waves, the clash of sword
On sword and sword on shield does stop
as the night descends so fast!

While they sleep, the injured and the lost, victors and defeated, all
On the same field, united in death and life,
a wind begins to blow a wall

A susurration that ripples across the field
like a wave, fast advancing tall
Grass, like a giant gliding across, picking up
spoils of war that anyone would gall.

When the morn does come, the skies are
flooded with birds as large as
Clouds, they circle round and round in
spirals and all the time, those that
Sleep, are shaken roughly by those that
wake, for none they see, naught
Of those that fell yesterday, all that remain
are empty spaces to the gaze.

Thus do they all fear to return to war, even
as the sun does travel the sky
For none would want to be claimed as the
spoils of war. Wearily they gather
Their tools of war, and without a backward
glance do depart from the field!
Winners, losers bound by fear, even as the
clouds do dance in a blue sky.

Ecstasy - Did it really last?

Did it really last, the moment he spent with a woman of the night,
Warm arms that turned cold by morning, ropes that choked him?
Ecstasy - A brief spell that passed away
leaving him empty and blank!
It leaves you wondering if it had been worth it if it did not last!

Did it really last, the high, that the bit of
weed given to her, to feel as
Though she ruled the world even though
a pauper she would be? The
Kick that the last puff gave her did wear
away in the morning. It left her
With a headache and emptiness wanting
more even as her mind did reel.

Did it really last, that banquet of free
flowing wine and endless platters
Of exotic food, setting them on a high,
only to end in an upset stomach,
Wanting to disgorge the kebabs and wine
that they had fed on the previous

Night? The cornucopia of pleasures did
　　leave them the next day in tatters!

Alas! The moment did pass; leaving them
　　to wonder if had been worth it,
A moment so brief that it left them wanting
　　for more, the applause, the
Clapping, the reviews, the praise of men
　　that worshipped them, all faded
Away, when alone they lay at the end of day,
　　emptiness that left them in a fit!

Like fireflies we flit - lights that last a night, even as we search for
　　Another high. Unfortunately it does not
　　last and we hunger for another
Kick that would sweep us to another realm,
　　far away from the drudge of
This world, even as we sip and dip into
　　pleasures deep to take us far.

Alas, the moment does pass leaving us
　　high and dry, to face the realities
As we count endless days! The ecstasy of the
　　moment does pass so fast, a flame
That consumes more than it feeds. For
　　surely I want a pleasure that lasts,
Grants, peace and contentment! But then they
　　don't last, these earthly pleasures!

The ecstasy and the kicks won't last a bit, after we wake at last,
The pleasures of the night fade away,
even as the day arrives, leaving
In us a hunger and a craving for more, an ecstasy that would last
Forever! But then these earthly pleasures really don't a bit last!

We do seek a moment to ease, the pain -
our companion of so many
Years, a divine ecstasy that would last, to
be intoxicated in the spirit and
Not the flesh the definitive moment, the
moksh a release from lesser pleasures
To partake of a divine cornucopia of joy
that would be an endless party.

Although of this Earth we are not in it, but
floating in a continuum of glory.
We are not of the soil that would feed our
interstices with intoxicating
Chemicals put our minds to sleep. We are
of the skies and of the spirits
That run the realms, the pleasures of the
flesh, therefore suffice us not!

A Requiem for Two

Even as the day does sink, the time to part draws near, the
Years of togetherness draw to an end, days, months, years;
The clock slows down to that final moment of parting, even as
You prepare for a final journey to a place in another realm !
Farewell, God speed both of you!

What remain are the times we shared,
laughs, tears, admonishments
Anecdotes and thoughts that'll remain for
ages to come, till we too leave
On our final journey, thus we wonder why
two brothers did set out on a
Journey so soon, and realise the one did
so, the other company to give!
Farewell, God speed both of you!

Though grief does fill our minds with thoughts of what might
Have been, time n tide stop for none as the sand that trickles
Down the glass. With prayers and best wishes we bid you a happy
Journey to new lands, peace and contentment be yours forever!
Farewell, God speed both of you!

With the two gone away from us, we can only wish that you
Find comfort in each other's company, knowing well that you
Were close to each other, and could not bear to be parted;
Two brothers who left within a gap of a month and seven days!
God speed both of you!

Two brothers did leave within a gap of one month and seven
Days, both eager to journey together, to meet loved ones in
The land of afterlife, where they meet their Maker who loves
Them the most, the elder would not let his younger go alone!
God speed both of you!

He would not let his brother go alone, so to be with him, and hold
His hand, he left this land and all of us,
a big brother to comfort one
Who might fear a dark journey on a lonely
night? The two are like stars
In a galaxy of a myriad stars, two stars that blaze a fiery trail across
The sky, God speed both of you!

For what can we say except that what the Lord has destined will
Come to pass, our grief knows no bounds, though the sight of the
Two stars flashing across the skies does bring a smile to our lips!
For bound by their love, united the travel,
to lands where He awaits!
Farewell, God speed both of you!

Farewell, God speed both of you, carry with you our prayers and
Wishes, we will remember you all our lives, and the good times
We shared with you! The good times must end as we must part
Our ways, better times will come when we meet again, till we
Meet fare you well, God speed both of you!

This poem was read out by the author as
a tribute to his uncle during his memorial
service exactly one month and seven days after
the author's father left for his heavenly abode.

A Roadside Barber

Click, click go the pair of scissors, parting
away the tenderly grown hair,
All as the world goes by, the mirror reflects
the busy road, the two, barber
And customer bound together in an intimate
relationship, even as the world
Passes by.

A barber's chair sits by the roadside, a
mirror hung on the trunk of a tree,
Scissors, razors, brush and towel arranged
on a table greet the curious
Eye. An intimate relationship it would be as
the man on the chair points out
At a pimple on his chin.

The barber like wise man advises his
customer about potions and lotions
That would the pimple take away! And I
wonder if the barber would have

Solutions for the problems of the world?
Politicians and Economists would
Do well to visit him!

For besides cutting hair and shaving his
beard, the roadside barber offers
Expert advice on family problems, office
problems, mistress problems and
Health problems, all as the world goes by!
So unconcerned, indifferent to the
To the world they sit barber and him!

So, though his chair be rickety and the
stuffing be lumpy and missing, the
Mirror tarnished, the leaves the roof and
world the room, it might after all,
Be the wise man's seat, where wisdom is
shared for a mere twenty, a shave
And a haircut e 'en as the world passes by!

Unconcerned of the world, barber and man, lost in a conversation,
Of greying, and thinning hair, of pimples
and issues of the world, even as the
Tree sheds its leaves, as though in
acknowledgement of a divine relationship,
Between the roadside barber and his client!

And I the mute spectator do watch the stillness
of a tableau, even as the traffic
Drives on, a glimpse of a scene so rich of
a roadside barber and his client,

A haircut followed by a shave, and invaluable
anecdotes of life such that I've never
Heard of even as the world passes by!

Click click go the scissors, as they shear the unwanted hair,
Rasp rasp goes the blade as it sunders unwanted hair, to make
The chin and cheek gleam with health and youth, oh for the magic
Of the roadside barber that I would not know!

And I, the silent spectator, would crane my neck to hear the secrets
Shared by the barber and his man, but alas the
secrets are denied to one who moves
With the world that passes on with a mind
of its own. The chair that awaits
The one to come, wisdom to share, and hair to cut!

Dawn

Aloft,   we rise,
Higher, and   higher on the thermals
         Warm to greet the day
   As we soar!

   Circling   In copper
Sky we climb   The stair to heaven
         And greet the
      The morning
   New

The
Sun glorious
Rises in distant horizon
A rosy-red glow blankets the sky
Even as a distant jet spins out a vapour-
Trail, stitching the sky in a long white thread
Drawing together two ends of the sky, the East
And the West, a golden-glow of love and promise
Of a fresh day and opportunities new! The morning
Brings with it the chance of a mistress relenting and
Saying, 'Yes!' - Being selected for a long wanted job
Or reconciliation with an angry brother! And the fresh
Breeze fills you with freshness, and the warm beams
Of the sun fills you with wonder and joy for the gift of
One more day, a renewed chance to mend anew,
One's own life and mistakes too! A moment to
Thank, a moment to praise, a moment to try
One last shot before the day does end,
And all the while, the birds do fly
To test the wind even as you
Gaze with wonder at the
Round copper
Sun.

The clouds do float in
The sky that glows, and shapes do form
Of men, animals, flowers and trees, a canvas vast,
By an artist so great! For God did create for you and me;
An inspiration for poet and scientist alike, cures
For the ills, solutions for litigation long!
Might you gain inspiration pure
Then greet the sun and praise
The Lord! Thus would you
Insight and wisdom
Gain.

And as the sun does rise,
Majestically in the sky,
The world does stir,
However, lazily. They all
Do and miss the magic of the rising
Sun! But laziness - None could benefit. Therefore
They turn a blind eye to
The magic of the morn!

Seven Hours

Just as I was about to go off to sleep, at ten in the
night, the Reaper came and said to me,
'You have seven hours to live, unless of course
you are able to identify the purpose to live,'
I went into a state of frenzy and turned my thoughts
here and there and wondered about the
Things I yet had to do before I left this world!
Thinking deeply, I gathered my classics thinking
That I should get a lead! However, I was in a frenzy
and thought I should bid my friends a
Farewell! I turned and looked at my family who
were sound asleep, so in despair I turned to
Facebook and greeted all my friend and bid them
farewell, but satisfied I was not, so I switched
To Twitter, but felt so hollow! By then, the hour turned
eleven and in a tizzy, I turned to my books!

The first book that I turned to in my mind was
Plato's Republic! I did not know where
I had put it, but then sat down and thought of what
I had read of it, and I remembered the allegory

Of the cave. What if we were really only living in a
world at a second remove? What if we were
Living in a world that is but a shadow of the real
world? If this world is but a thought dreamed by
Someone, are we only players in a drama thought
out by one who creates a world like a play
To play a drama that enacts a life of shadows and
dreams? And so I thought on and on, knowing
Well that it was eleven in the night, one hour minus
the seven hours that I would live unless
Of course I could tell the Reaper about the
meaning of my life on this Earth!

It was twelve in the night, that magical moment
between life and death, the twilight that
Is neither of the living and the dead, and I turned
my thoughts to the people I had once
Known, my grandmother, my aunt who had been
full of life but cut short by cancer, and I
Wondered if I had been blessed more than
them! I turned to the pile of books to
Look for an answer to the dilemma that the
reaper had put to me. The book that I
Had in hand was Plautus's Pot of Gold. I read
the lines, 'I shall be the happiest man
In the world, instead of the most miserable,
which is what I have been ever since it
Came into my possession.' I thought of all
the money that I had put into my
Savings, but it gave me no relief, and I
wondered if I could buy a few hours!

It was one O clock and I was really wild, there
were only four hours left before
The Reaper would come for me, therefore, I
turned to my next book hoping that
It would give me some idea about the purpose
of my life in this world. I turned to
Homer's Odyssey, and this is what I read
in desperation trying to find
The secret of the purpose of my life on this
planet, for surely I did not want to
Leave so early in what I thought to be the
prime of my life, though I was stepping
Into my late forties! Well this is I read, 'my heart
is in some perplexity...I am alone, whereas
They are always together in a crowd,' I wondered
about the friends that would not
Respond to my calls. I wondered if I was alone
in my quest for the truth to free me!

It was two in the morning and they were fast
asleep, not wishing to disturb them,
I turned to my next book, for answers I was
desperate to know and sure enough,
I lay my hands on A collection of Old Indian Legends
by Zitkala-Sa, and I wondered if I could find
The purpose of life before I slipped into another
realm and this is what I got 'To ride on one's
Own feet is tiresome, but to be carried like a warrior
from a brave fight is great fun!' So it is
But fine to have lived as a warrior from a brave
fight although I guess this would mean
A fight not necessarily with guns and sticks,
but of principles and justice, to make

A stand against falsehood and wrongdoings. I
turned towards ever growing pile of books
And decided which book to take up next. And
my eyes fell on to a book covered in blue.
Sighing, I picked up that book, even as the relentless
time flowed away like fine grains of sand.

It was by now three in the morning and I in
the dead still of the night was more
Alive than ever as I searched for the purpose
of life. And so I turned to the Gita for
Insight and answers and thus I read, 'Those great souls who love
Me, and (out of love for me) merge in my
spirit, achieve the highest success.
They need never return again to this ephemeral,
grief stricken world.' And thus
I could see that the true purpose of life
is not personal success or self-
Glory, but to merge into the greater Soul. But
how could I do that, for all I knew
I had spent my whole life running after
success, and praise, and money and
Fame! Fearing that my time was come, I
knelt down to pray for guidance,
For the test to pass was all I wanted. And
in my prayer, a voice directed me
To another book, buried in the midst of
an ever growing pile of books.

When I opened my eyes, it was there, in front
of me, I had not seen it before!
The Holy Bible was its title, and I opened a
random page to see if something

I could get from it, and this is what I got, 'It
is through Faith that all of you are
God's own in union with Christ Jesus....And
Since you are his son, God will give you
All that he has'. I rejoiced on reading these words
and wondered if it was faith that I lacked!
But then voices of doubt and suspicion rang
in my ears, 'You have only three
Hours left before he comes, why do you waste
your time reading books?' But I thought
Perhaps I might get the answer to the riddle of
the purpose of life and so I answered,
'Let go, get lost, for I need to find answers, and all I
know is that they are hidden in these books!'
The voices quieted and I looked at the clock
and it was four in the morning.

I sweated and panicked for I just an hour left,
the voice Faith said to me, 'Why don't
You kneel down again and pray to The Almighty
Lord for forgiveness? You despaired
And forgot your Maker, for what are these
books but thoughts of men, why not talk
To Him that made them think?' Prompted, I
thought of Plato and what he said of reality
In his allegory of the cave and once again on my
knees I dropped! And time flew faster,
My last hour drew near, but I knew it not till
the alarm rang five, and a sweet voice
Spoke into my ears, 'Wake up son, it is time
to go, unless of course you have the
Answers!' I lifted my head and smiled at her
said to her, the reaper, 'I have no

Fear of death, for there is no such thing as
death, for purpose of life is but to
Celebrate eternity, and spread the message of
faith! To fight a battle with doubt
And despair befits a warrior, for the battle is
fought not with sword, but the conviction
That life and death are only transitions,
mere gateways to the infinite!'

I woke up to a bright morning, and saw all
my people around me, of the books
I saw none except that they were in their places
in the bookshelf! I went to each one
Of them and brushed my hands lightly
against them, and marvelled about
The dream I had had! I looked around me and
saw the things I collected throughout
My years, I saw nothing but bits and pieces,
and they meant nothing to me,
My books I cherished and the people around
me I embraced. In my mind Life
Had another meaning and I tightened my
belt and set out on my battle to fight
Despair and doubt, with Faith beside me, and
a new purpose before me! Yonder
In the sky I saw a figure beckon to me,
as if telling me to pick up my
Staff and follow him. Obeying a voice that
told me to fight the good fight,
I went around and told my friends and
neighbours about this vision of mine!

A Steadying Hand

Dear Lord, you held me up when I was falling, when
I was sad and fearful about how to tackle my tasks,
But You handled them so well that the day
Did pass as smooth as silk! What would I do
But for you, my Lord, my stanchion and my staff!

The day looms ahead with doubt and insecurity but
As I kneel down in prayer begging for your help, I
Feel the strength flowing through me, even when
I feel lost and confused! You raised up so that the
Moment did pass as smooth as silk with you by my side!

And so I carry on, lost and confused, drifting, but for
For your guiding touch O lord my God, you have
Been my companion throughout and I shall not want
Another! You hold me up in the face of adversity and tribulation,
So I shall not stumble even though the path might be rocky!

You hold me up when my spirit is weak and I am surrounded
By tribulations and doubts; the path is long twisted and dark, the
Shadows blanket me on each step. The night does come and

I am lost, but you show me a light at the other end of the
Dark path, to perk me up and lead me to salvation!

O lord my God, but for you, I would lie down and let the
Sands of despair engulf me, but then your voice does
Wake me up before the storm does reach me, to seek shelter
In your arms that embrace me, and protect me from the
Vagaries of fate and uncertain times.

Dear Lord, you hold me up on your shoulders as strong
As the mountains that stand aloft and
challenge the ocean of despair,
In storms of despair, you are so resolute, firm
and stable! For what am I but a lost
Lamb that seeks to find its way through a
path beset with the rocks of doubt,
And treacherous rocks? But you guide
me on till I reached my home!

So my Lord my God, you hold me up, lest
I drown in the sea of despair,
A soft hand that comforts me so! And
when my feet teeter and falter,
Your steadying touch guides me on to the winding path that passes
Through the darkness, a light that glows ahead, a voice that calls.
So it is but a light touch that holds me on till I reach my home!

Voices of Freedom

Liberated they fly into the morning sky - a myriad spirits that
Flit across the molten sky, shrieking and screaming of things done
Wrong - protests and complaints drowned in anguished flight!

As skies do burn bright and hot, birds do spin before the fire
Round and round, though the heat does singe. Like moths
Drawn to flame (though they burn), and forms a growing pyre!

A thousand tortured souls do rise, to protest of life not fair, for
Having promising lives cut short by blast so rude, lives cut short
In prime of life, if only they'd be brought back by tears and prayer!

For what manner of men could dare – to
rend asunder, sweet delicate
Bonds of love, lovers hand in hands, a mother smiling at her babe
Poet writing to his creator, all in one rude
second, split and rent through hate!

A thousand tortured souls do rise to protest
of iniquities of life not fair,
And as the sun does rise, liberated they fly into the sky,
And wonder aloud of reasons that make men rend asunder!

The sky does burn with fire so bright, eyes
do burn with light so bright!
A thousand stars flit around a fire that burns
white and red, and as they fly, a wailing
Does rise, a cry of despair and hope so lost.
If only … if only God would right!

And as the sun in size does grow, a taper to
light a thousand souls, they come
With anger and wail so loud, that ear
would burst with sound so loud!
And yet the day, so sure does come, a taste of things yet to come.

Another day of fear and hunger dawns, filled
with pain, anguish and suffering;
Of children torn from parents, and women
taken before their men, of men shot

Before their sons, a blood-sport fit to
fill the sewers with anything!

With eyes open, yet senses closed, their
neighbours they see, dragged
To charnel houses to feed the hate, while with
hearts that beat they wait to flee,
The beasts that hunger to feed on emotions so sweet!

With hearts that beat they wait to flee,
advancing beast that wish to feed
On feelings and emotions that are so
tender. But even as they try to fly,
They are swatted to the ground for hogs to feed!

Alas they become but part of a stat, mere numbers
To feed a beast of hate, that trolls for victims so to feed
A machine on blood and feelings that runs!

So take to flight all souls that care, lest you
should melt with shame and plight,
For humanity does stay the hand that slays,
alas, alas, the cruel hand won't await
A mother's sweet smile and the glance
of love, the wrong to right!

So rent the sky with screams so loud, and
flood the plains with tears
So deep, fill the plains with remorse so
great, for what have we done to
Weep so deep? Enough is enough, so
stop the hate, the flow of tears!

So stop the killings, and the shriek of tortured
souls, the myriad souls that flit
The skies, so hear the sweet songs of love
and care, for tears that weigh
so deep! Let us create a world so fair, with love to fill a world so fit!

So let us free the souls from the hate that sweeps the world,
And teach the world of love and sacrifice, and the smile
Of love that transcends all hatred, in a beautiful world!

And so as they wheel around a final time, before the sky
Does swallow them, they cry out one last time for freedom,
From:
Pain and suffering,
Bombs and guns,
And those that hurt,
Unfeeling minds,
That rend asunder,
Mother and child,
And sweet hearts that cling!

Dragon's Tail

The dragon lies in his lair, belching smoke and flames,
And when he steps out of his cave, he endeavours
To cover his cowering minions with dust covered wings,
'Sure I am the prince of confusion, Lucifer incarnate' and
Flaps the stubs of his wings as he lets out a belch of
Rotten flesh and food gone bad!

All the while his minions cowering do lie, glancing at
This amazing apparition, a little man, a
beggar in tattered rags does bat
With his staff at the serpent's tail of the fiery dragon, and at
Once does the dragon gasp in pain as his tail does quiver with
The insult of one so humbled! 'Why dost thou to render me
So weak before the minions that cower before me?'

And even as he throbs with pain and ego hurt so bad, the
Dragon does slip into his lair so dark, to lighten the
Slight that offended so! And all the while do minions the
Offence do salve, but as they slip into the lair with the stench
Are greeted! And as the mighty dragon does see his minions,
With cracking jaws and rumbling stomach he rolls around!

And even as he covers his shame with anger
to blame, his tail does sweep
The air around even as weak, pathetic
minions do scurry for cover so deep,
The evil tail does seek the gathered throng.
A deep rumble does seep
Through the parted lips, how did one with
scaly neck fall so fast! But where
Did one with tattered rags flee so fast? An
insult he delivered none too nice!
And thus does groan, the prince of confusion
gnashing his fangs on empty air.

And so advances the mighty dragon, fiery
and livid, but with a shrivelled tail
That hangs with shame. Others would laugh
that he drags his ego so hurt, a wail
Of pain from twisted throat does creep! And
as the one who support did wail
As the dust of crushed flesh bones he
sailed to fall into a pit of defiled
Filth, all smeared with his lord's scum, 'O
prince of confusion, why do you
Gnash your teeth, for surely have I treated you with care?'

But then with a mighty belch of flames
does the heart of mighty beast
Shrivel to naught, with hurt so deep! His sting does miss the feast
Of grovelling minions with souls so weak,
what would happen to the least
Of least even as they see their Lord smitten
by one so weak? And as they

See their prince of confusion eaten up by
his own doubts, they scurry to
Escape the end of their lives even as the cave mouth does shut!

Thus do the minions and their Lord coil
over each other in slug fest
Of corruption and stink so bad that should the odours escape past
The sealed lips of the lair, befuddled and would others be. Lost
And wandering, doddering fools that evil would embrace, even as
Their Lord does belch the noxious fumes.
But all the while does the
Beggar outside pluck the strings of his instrument!

With a final loud bang does the door shut down
on the mighty Dragon and his host
A parody of his old self, brought down by a
beggar with robes torn and scarf lost
He wills himself to sing songs of battles
won, but alas, this one he has lost!
He tries to rest even as the sun does sink,
to remind him of the battle,
Not with force, but modesty so profound, that you and me did treat
With the story of the mighty dragon brought down by one so weak!

But then, as the sun does sink, to my bed I needs must go, for
Time is so short, and the games that people do play for
Times that come, of devious minds that innocent souls for
Breakfast do claim even as they wait for the night to dawn!
However, the mighty dragon, one last bellow does release,
To claim what is not his but then I guess it's time to get up!

The dragon's not yet done, and as the stone does roll over
The cave's entrance, he shouts, 'how dare you claim the cover

Of being devout when all that matters is
the power that I would deliver
The power that you would want, women and wine and joys of life,
To smother one and all, for I am the prince
of confusion, Lucifer brought down
With a scorpion's tail and sting so sharp
that your senses it would dull!'

But then the cave's entrance has been shut so tight, so close,
Even while the beggar outdoors strums his instrument so close
To his chest even as the dragon and his
minions in sleeping death do doze,
With opiates that mind do dull, and while
they wait for their lord to wake,
With baited breath they wait for scraps to
throw, and kingdoms big or small,
Satisfied they'd be, with gifts to shame for
souls they've sold to flatter one.

Even as the prince of deep does in deep
sleep complain of powers lost
In a cave so dark, he lies, waiting to feed on
feeble minds in a world so lost.
The contented do sleep, others do dream of
power to keep and wars to boast!
And while the sun does speed, and clouds do
crawl stings do seek for prey new!
Imprisoned, abandoned, he lies in dungeon
so dark waiting and waiting,
For fools to come and fetch him out, for
stench of rot makes him so sick!

Words

Words are like building blocks that a structure create!
The right choice of words would a message create
Of images sharp and ideas clear, to remove blunders
That cause an embarrassment so sure!

Of verbs I know that actions describe, and nouns so
Dear that name my friends, adjectives so
Fair that define my friends and prepositions
So pat that make positions so clear!

The linkers I know that connect all I know, verbs and
Nouns and sentences that flow, to remove the clutter and bind
The structure that I make, for all to see! For I would not like
To ramble on, but to Convey message all so clear.

And to cement my words with dancing words,
I use participles and gerunds
And play with past participles because
I would not like to end my action so!

My prepositions I use so fans should hang from ceilings.
While I pour tea into my cup, ideas I place in sentences

That glow, and so I dive into rules that confuse me so,
Thus, Will I walk a mile with you if it pleases you so

Of adjectives I know, that the red ball pleases you so,
For you are a good friend and I like you so!
And if a short lesson in rules would please you,
A lesson crisp I will share with you.

Modals I would give, as advice to help you,
For I dare not leave alone one so innocent like you,
For When in Rome you must obey the elders -
In Greece you ought to visit the Parthenon!

The Great Blame Game

They claim to be experts in their field but bungle
When responsibilities are given, they fumble,
But are raring to play a blame game!

They claim to be hard working and try look busy
While doing nothing, they carry books too many,
That they claim they are checking!

And all the time they spend in gossip as they tear
To pieces the one in charge, as they bear
The burden of what they call is work too much!

They gang up when the egg falls on their faces,
Wiping faces they try to regain lost places,
For they are adept in the great blame game!

The one who seeks to lead would love to be mother hen,
And her smile is worse than her bite as she gathers her mien!
For to hound her superior is her game!

And all who gather around her are hunters that gather for a kill,
E'en as her followers gather to share the kill!
As the post blames them for their ineptitude!

'You did not tell us, nor did you inform us!' They screech
As in one voice they deliver all for all a speech!
For so they think it would deliver their coup de grace!

Even as they play the great blame game for things not done,
But then, I guess they would be wracked with guilt as one,
For the ineptitude of those who play a game!

And as the mother hen does gather the chicks under her wing,
She gathers strength from those that consent for a fling,
And so she shuffles her feathers, (the few
that remain), as she struts her thing!

Like minor dogs do the wag their tails when under their leader
They gain shelter! But then I feel they need a feeder
To fill their empty minds even as they play the blame game.

An Ode to Twilight

Part I

The sun has sunk and cannot see, yet the clouds
   do glow with pinks and reds. The sky
Out East turns thick and dark, but the East does
   glow with eerie light, that bathes the
World with calm so deep, to keep, at bay the
   shadows that creep; one last burst of
Light so bright, before day submits to fairies
   fair! Thus, do watch man and beast with
Baited breath, that dare not break the magic
   that flows, from West to East, a sight to
See by one and all! And so, when the day has
   gone, the sky does blaze with muted light,
That keeps away the shadows that grow, e'en
   as the night awaits, her turn to grow!

Thus bodies so weary wait to sleep, a day so
   long of toil and roil; when martial minds
Swords do still (that cut asunder lovers that hunger),
   the pen does fall from fingers that tire

While scribes do wait to see a funder! The general
does wait to plot asunder, a victory sure
To blast a thunder. The twilight does cast
spells of wonder, a magic feast to treat
A hunger. And as the sun does sink a wink,
the heavens do light a world so bright.
But none would wait to miss a spell, of light and
might, and plight of sight – while I do
Write of light so fair, of sight so bright, a twilight
to light a mind to write of life so trite.

The twilight's a time that stops all hands, minds
that work and feet that toil, enthralled by
Fate, magic so great, the King does wait at cusp
so late, to try his weight to claim so
Late, a throne to date, a reign to save. The eagle
does dive to claim his bait, as all do wait
To see the stake. The twilight does come, oh, so
late, the date to fate, when all is late, so
Caught to date, for moment to wait as 'Xander
on his bight, did wait for turn of fate, for
Time to come, but all he sees are sprites so late
as they fly from light so late. And so does
Glow the sky to lave, minds that wait for dreams
to sate, empty lives that turn and wait!

Part II

As the glow the world does lave, he knows so
clear another dawn he'll never see!
So strange t'was that Socrates did see, the truth
that struck the heart so sharp, the
Answer he sought was there to see, in twilight
hour before he sank, answer made so
Plain and Clear in time so short, as light does
gleam; on earth so vast, a balm for eyes
And limbs that pine, a rest, a feast, for those
that hunger, but dare not pause, lest the
Road not end. Thus do traveller and warrior
glance askance, at sky that burns with
Light so strange; the clouds do turn, pink
and red, copper and purple, while
The road does lead the two to where welcome
lights do glow, and hearth awaits.

They waste their lives away looking for answers
and meanings of life, but then, Alas!
It flashes so late in moment short, in blink of
eye, if only you would pause and wait, to
Watch the light that casts away, the shadow of
night, despair so tight, t'is all written in
Twilight clear, if life would be only of success
and failure, where then would be the rest?
What matters not is success or victory, but to see
so clear, the sky aglow, so pause awhile
Oh traveller and general, to see the sky that
lights beyond, the day's not done, the
Night's not come, the sky does cast a spell so
great, for all that pause for sight so grand!

Part III

If only they'd stay awhile - to gaze at a spell so
     great, a sight so grand, a glory so bright,
For by the end what matters so clear is to pause
     awhile and drink the sight, a moment
So clear, when sun does sink, the light does stay
     to light the night. And as the traveller
Does rush to reach hearth and home, the earth
     does glow with hope and joy, a glee writ
Large, with magic so fair, and balm so fine, a sight
     to feed the eyes that pine for light that
Heals! And ears that tire might hear the songs, of
     love so true, and truth so fair, as fairies
Do surf the skies that light, (a sight so grand)
     and smile at those that deign to look!

If light be life and dark be death, twilight does
     stand between the both, a moment of
Truth for the philosopher that hungers, the poet
     does gain words so strange, (those that
Slipped his fingers) the general does gain the
     secret to victory, the man his mistresses'
Embrace - all united in a moment so great, as the
     sun does sink, the night awaits, twilight
Does pass-a reign of languor and cloying love,
     sweet with love and passion to seal the
Union with kisses and hugs, the lovers that pined
     for moment so rich, and as they lie on
Couches that float, with pillows so soft, the night
     approaches so calm with breeze so soft.

Part IV

The pinks and reds, copper and blood do transfix
artist and bureaucrat, alike. So deep
As the shadows do grow, the skies do glow with
energy so bright, a final blaze, to herald
The passing away of a day gone by, another to
come. A moment so calm, that destructive
Minds, it stills with smiles and love so sweet. Great
minds it drove to think of mysteries so
Deep, of life so true, when mothers do pause to
lull the crying, when despots do pause to
Smile at least? And as I gaze at the twilight sky,
I lose myself in magic so deep, even as
The traffic does speed by with a mind of its own,
I scream to it to pause for a moment!

And while I wail for all to pause, the twilight
does spread bathing the world in light,
A light so deep that it would battle the street
lights so dull. Magic does come for those
That pause, alas, none do wait for the magic
that is, the twilight does come
And pass away, a moment so deep and yet so short,
if only they'd a moment pause and be!
And as the day does come to stop, the glow
does bathe a world so vast, as I do
Rest my head so dull, I watch the skies that glow,
with light so deep, and wait and watch
The sky that burns, farewell my dears till we
meet, in days to come and miles to come.
Just wait and watch oh traveller so weary, for
twilight does spell a message so deep!